Luigi Guicciardi

Inspector Cataldo's Criminal Summer

Translated from the Italian by Iain Halliday

 Hersilia Press

First published in Great Britain in 2010
by Hersilia Press, Oxfordshire
www.hersilia-press.co.uk

© Luigi Guicciardi
English Translation © Iain Halliday

Originally published 1999 in Italy as *La Calda Estate del Commissario Cataldo* by Edizioni Piemme S.p.A, Milano

The right of Luigi Guicciardi to be identified as the author of this work has been asserted.

Printed in Great Britain by
the MPG Books Group, Bodmin and King's Lynn

CHAPTER ONE

The meeting

It is only the end of June and it is already too hot in Guiglia. At ten in the morning the windows of the houses shine in the sun, and the glare is stronger than it should be. It is holiday time – the schools are closed, the kids are all out on their bikes every day. But right now there is a strange silence in the almost lazy, somnolent air, in the few hotels that are open, in the streets, in the calm, in the light.

And in Via Dante Alighieri there is a detached house that seems immersed in the quiet. Apart that is from two voices – one shrill, the other low – that debate and dispute rhythmically, each filling the other's pauses with a subtle, hidden tension.

'I know we're meeting tomorrow morning, we've got that appointment, and I could have left it till then,' says the younger one. 'But I thought you might want some idea of what I've found beforehand. And I thought you might be able to give me some advice...'

'That's alright, Giulio. Have I ever said no to you? So...'

'That's why I asked you to come over,' continues Giulio Zoboli, slightly uneasy. 'You know, since you're in Guiglia and the university's closed...'

'It's fine,' says the other man, cutting Zoboli short with a gesture. 'I've already told you that. So, let's see it...'

'Here, this is everything I've gathered so far,' and he pushes a large canvas-bound notebook across the desk, towards the professor. Then he smiles, shy and proud at the same time, while the older man puts on his glasses and starts leafing through the notebook, concentrating, almost as though he does not understand.

'It looks like a big job,' he says, reading through the pages filled with tiny handwriting. Then he falls silent and waits.

'I've been working on it for three months, right up to the day before yesterday. It's all unpublished correspondence, as you said, and all of it with important intellectuals – Croce, Gentile, Pirandello...' He stops, as though studying the effect of his words on the other man, almost savouring it. 'There's even a letter from Joyce.'

'Really?' He perks up, almost starts, but manages to conceal his excitement. 'Good. And can we reconstruct the corre-spondence?' as he stares at Zoboli. 'I mean, both sides...'

'Oh yes. Almost all of it. Formiggini built up a fine archive in his thirty years as a publisher, and he kept everything in there: originals of letters from other people and carbon copies of his replies. That's the good thing about it.'

'A real treasure trove.' He nods, but without smiling, almost as though he is thinking about something else. Indeed, a moment later he adds, 'By the way. Did you find out if anyone has seen this material before?'

'No one, I'm sure of it. The director of the Estense Library assures me I'm the first.'

'Good. And tell me,' pointing to the pages of the notebook, 'how did you work on it?'

'As you can see, I copied the most interesting parts of all the letters, naturally in chronological order, from some thir-ty sets of correspondence – the most promising ones based on the name of the correspondent. And of course I copied some of the more important letters in their entirety. This one here, for example...'

He stands up and moves round the desk until he is beside

the professor, bending over slightly and pointing to a page.

'A 1913 letter from Momigliano. He was due to edit an edition of Porta's *Ninetta del Verzé*, but then he got cold feet.' He thinks, pauses. 'The letter's very... how shall I put it?'

'Awkward?'

'Well... no, let's say delicate. There were some problems regarding censorship, back in those days. Pornography...'

'And do you think it's important?'

'This one is, definitely. It goes beyond his personal situation and throws some light on a slice of life in terms of national customs...'

'At the beginning of the century. Right.'

The professor reads a few lines in silence. Then he lifts his gaze to his assistant, purses his lips in reflection and in approval.

'Good. Very good.'

'And that's not all,' Zoboli says, as he goes back behind the desk, encouraged now as he opens a drawer and pulls out a sheaf of pages, stapled together.

'This is the paper. What you've got there is all the material in the notebook, isn't it? The transcriptions of the letters, the texts... lots of them. This is the conclusion.' He looks into his eyes, almost euphoric. 'The verdict...'

'Let's have a look...'

He takes the pages, reads a few sentences, then he stops, stares for a moment at Zoboli in silence, adjusts his glasses and continues reading in earnest. When he finishes he takes off his glasses and places them on the sheets of paper, rubbing his tired eyes.

'I think it'll do.'

The glasses are for long-sightedness and have heavy, unfashionable frames, making him look older than he is.

And Luigi Ramondini is not that old, not much older than his assistant. He has just turned forty-three and only recently become full Professor of Italian Literature at Bologna University. Zoboli is forty, and works for Ramondini, on temporary contracts.

'A good job well done. Yes. There's just one thing... I have to tell you something. I didn't mention it before because I only found out yesterday...'

There are deep lines running from the professor's nose towards his cheeks, making his face seem sculpted into a grin.

'They want me to present the paper. The people on the organizing committee. They want a big name, so to speak... more academic authority, you see. That's the thing. There's no other reason.'

'And what did you say?'

'There wasn't much I could say. I tried to tell them there was someone already working on it... under my direction I mean, and that this person was keen to present the paper at the conference. But it didn't do any good.'

'But you'd promised.'

'No, you can't say I promised. I didn't promise you anything, you obviously misunderstood. I only told you there was a chance of working on something new, on unpublished manuscripts with good prospects for publication. Nothing more. I never mentioned the conference, you just interpreted it that way.' He is huffing now, getting angry. 'You really ought to start listening to people sometimes, instead of just hearing your own voice.'

'So it's my fault then? Here we go again! First you tell me to work hard, that it'll be worthwhile because the *concorso* is coming up and this would be an extra qualification which might help me win a job in it this time... and that you'll give me advice and all the rest. And I take it all on board, I work like nobody's business for three months, turning down a supply teaching job and then you come along, fresh as a daisy, to tell me I'm the one who misunderstood, and that they've decided I'm not good enough... but what do they care who wrote it, if the paper's good?'

'Listen, it's not my fault. This isn't Delfini, the writer you wrote that book about, the book few people have actually read. This is new research, I mean... they want guarantees...'

'Exactly! And what better guarantee than you!'

'Don't start with the sarcasm now. I understand, really I do. You're the one who's done all the work...'

'Thanks so much...'

'But you have to see my side too. Again, it's not my fault. But that's the way things stand,' and he opens his arms as he adds, 'and there's nothing I can do about it.'

'That's right, nothing. And you'll use all this,' pointing to the papers and the notebook, 'just like that, without even an acknowledgment... because you get the money and all the credit. It's already decided, isn't it?'

His voice had become high-pitched, even squeaky, and now that he has finished, his face red, there are traces of saliva at the corners of his mouth.

'It's up to you. If you want to leave all this with me – and I'm not making any secret of the fact that it'll help me in writing up the paper – I can tell you that from this very moment on I am truly grateful to you...'

'Don't mention it.'

'Only if you want to, of course...'

'And if I don't want to?'

The other man is very calm when he replies, 'Well, I'll take this opportunity to remind you that at the end of this year the *concorso* for research jobs will be taking place and you're in the running, you've been in the running for some years... and I'm on the panel, as you well know...'

He looks at Zoboli, who is silent now, and continues: 'And as you also know, you won't be the only one competing. We'll see who's got the most publications, a PhD, or other things... the marks for the written exam and the oral, marks from the panel. From me too of course...'

'What is this? A threat?'

He smiles slightly, as he searches for the words. 'Why put it like that? I'd say it's more of a warning. I always like to forewarn people. Particularly those with whom I have, or could have, an official working relationship. But only after the competition...'

He smiles again as he lets the topic peter out, but perhaps it is precisely because of that smile that something clicks in the other man, a pent-up anger, perhaps, or that indefinable, subtle tension, a resentment that is already stale, something he has been carrying around within himself for some time.

'You think you've got me in the palm of your hand, don't you? You've got me with my back to the wall. But just be careful, Professor. Be careful because I know something about you, remember? Something that perhaps no one else should ever know...'

Now it is Ramondini who stares, without interrupting this time. He gets to his feet, slightly rigid, his knuckles turning white as he grips the edge of the desk.

'And there's nothing you can do about that, either. Because it has all already happened and you did quite well out of it... very well if I may say so.'

Perhaps he would have added something else, or the other

man would have spoken, and they would have raised their voices, both of them, in that isolated house, with no one to disturb them. But suddenly they were both stock still, looking each other in the eye, startled.

'What was that?'

A noise had come in through the open window looking out onto the garden. Sharp and metallic and nearby. Giulio, in his shirt sleeves with two circles of sweat under his armpits, goes to look. He leans out, turns his head right to left, while the man behind him doesn't move. Then he shakes his head, closes the window and turns back, stopping in the middle of the room.

'No-one. I wonder...'

Ramondini nods, his hands in his pockets. He opens his mouth to speak, then he thinks better of it and says nothing. He looks at the closed window, just beyond Giulio's shoulders and the sheets of paper and the notebook open on the desk. Then, slowly, he extends his hand and picks everything up, staring at Giulio, who makes no protest. The papers rustle slightly as Ramondini puts them in his briefcase. Giulio remains motionless as he watches him leave, without even a goodbye, his steps muffled in the entrance. He can show himself out.

CHAPTER TWO

The stranger

It is midday and it is warmer now. The sun is now cooking the bricks of the houses in the centre of Guiglia but in the Hotel Bandieri the air conditioning manages to keep everyone cool, partly because there are not many people there, just the regulars, since it is not yet high season. Cheese sandwich in the right hand, sports pages spread out between coffee cups and glasses of Pinot, eyes glued to the headlines – the clerks from Rolo Banca on their lunchbreak are easy to spot. But no one recognizes the man who enters now, looking for a room.

'Signor... ?'

'Alberto Ferrero.'

Two or three faces turn, then resume their positions and continue studying their newspapers. Ferrero has a moustache, he is tall and thin, good looking even, in a way, because of his green eyes, but no one is interested in that. All he has with him is a small bag.

'I've got a single room, right above us here. It should be alright, it's up to you...' And since the other man says nothing, he adds, 'I mean, it depends on how long you want it for...'

'It'll do fine,' and he moves to pull something out of his trouser pocket, his wallet of course, but the owner stops him nonchalantly.

'Don't worry, in your own good time. Go on up to your room if you want. I'll take your details and ID later,' and he lifts a numbered key off the panel on the wall. 'I guess you'll want to have a rest, what with this heat...'

The man nods as he takes the key.

'Of course, it's not always like this... I'm just telling you because you're a stranger here and you might have been expecting some cool weather.' He pauses before adding, 'Because you're not from round here: your voice makes that clear. I bet you're from quite some distance away...'

'From Turin.'

'There you go. That's what I'd have guessed. It's your accent...' And he takes a better look at Ferrero's profile as he is leaning over to pick up his bag. 'Of course, sunshine has its advantages. Not for me, though, I weigh a ton and I just sweat all day. But for anyone who's looking for a suntan, it's great.' He smiles, emphasizing his reference to the man's complexion, but Ferrero does not rise to it and goes up the stairs. The stranger really is very pale, a milky sort of pale, almost as though he is ill. Or as though he is afraid of the sun.

Ferrero comes back down and there is still a clerk or two with their noses in the newspaper, and the owner is still behind the walnut counter. He does not have his bag now and he is wearing a jacket and tie, even though it is still tremendously hot. He looks around and then heads for the reception counter, almost reluctantly. He already knows that the fat guy is not the best person to give him the information he is looking for, but what can he do? He needs help.

'How can I help you?'

He is standing behind the counter, his legs spread, hands behind his back, belly protruding. He has nothing to do but lift up all that fat on his tiptoes, every now and then letting it all fall back onto his heels before starting over again after a while.

'I'm looking for a colleague, Dr Giulio Zoboli. I've come to Guiglia to see him.'

'And don't you have his address?' he smiles, almost nastily.

It was obvious: this guy likes to ask questions instead of answering them.

'Of course I have an address, but one in Modena. I went there this morning and the neighbours told me he was here on holiday.' He stares convincingly. 'I didn't even know where Guiglia was. And I can't find him in the directory.'

'Because he's under Russo, of course.' He smiles again, indulgently, slightly surprised by such ignorance. 'The telephone's in his wife's name – Miriam Russo.'

'I don't know her.'

'Strange. They've been married for so many years you really should know her. They've been together ever since they started coming to the villa, in the summer and for weekends. And they don't have children, did you know that?'

'Me? No.'

'That's strange too. And yet you're friends.'

'Not friends. Colleagues.'

'Oh yes, you mentioned. Well, anyway, he's nearby. Via Dante Alighieri, at the bottom of the road. It's a detached house, with a nice garden. You really can't miss it... spitting distance. Out of here, up to the arch on Via Roma, go through it and then turn right, along Via Monteolo...'

The fat guy really is on the ball, but he has an ugly accent. And there is a sort of guttural sound to his voice, too, as though he were clearing his throat and about to spit with every sentence.

'Are you going there straight away?'

Ferrero looks at him, then shakes his head without speaking.

'I mean, if you go now you're sure to find him at home.'

'No, I'll have a beer first.'

The hotelier looks at him, disappointed, then turns to get a bottle from the refrigerated display, takes the top off and hands it to him with a glass, without pouring it.

'Here's the beer. Anything else?'

He stares. 'Yes, I just want to drink it in peace.'

The other man nods, but without blushing, and says, 'I see... I see.' Then he walks out from behind the counter with a tray to pick up the glasses and the cups and the paper napkins from the tables, stealing glances at Ferrero now and then, until Ferrero finishes the beer and leaves through the light that enters the room for a moment as the door opens, reflecting brightly on the shining floor. He exits with a slightly swinging gait, his jacket buttoned up, a bit tight on his hips, and a strange bulge in the pocket on his right side. The owner goes back behind his counter, picks up the register, studies the name for some time, studies the signature and continues to stare as though by doing so he might make some sense of it.

'Looks fake to me,' he concludes. And he thinks again about the man's pale complexion and tries to guess why and realizes that he spoke very little, that he kept his jacket buttoned up even though it is so hot, almost as though he wanted to hide something... 'Maybe he's a killer?' he says in the end, speaking to himself, his hoarse voice cracking. And now in his mind he sees a pistol in that pocket, and he is less curious, more worried.

The stranger does nothing strange. In no hurry, he walks along the roads, looking around as he goes, buys himself a newspaper and reads it for a while on the bench in Via

Monteolo, like a tourist. Every now and then he looks at the time, stretches his arms, starts walking again. It is almost four o'clock when he reaches the end of Via Dante Alighieri and there before him at number two is the villa. He stops opposite by a wall covered with old posters and studies the house with approval as he lights a cigarette. Then he leans his shoulders against the wall, studies the gate from a distance and exhales cigarette smoke with a sigh, either of satisfaction or of tiredness, and the few people around at that moment do not even think to look at him. He watches, feigning indifference, but without hiding himself. He could wait for him somewhere else, he thinks, not right outside his house, but a bit further away, even at the end of the road, at the corner with Via Parioli. But he stays put.

Quarter past four, twenty past four. He stands clear of the wall now and walks a bit further on until he comes to a bench. Still standing, he leans on the backrest with his elbows, feeling the heat from the sun. He looks at the road in the bright light and his eyes struggle to cope with the glare that suffuses the motionless, windless air. Then he yawns, stretches again, takes another drag from his cigarette. And his eyes now close to two slits because the sun is too much, then all of a sudden he puts his dark glasses on. In the silence he has just heard a metallic squeaking and he watches the gate open and a man walk out.

Zoboli looks around before crossing the road. And for a moment he even looks at the man with the dark glasses, without recognizing him, the man with invisible eyes and his lips in a straight, rigid line. Ferrero does not call out or say hello. He just nods almost imperceptibly, as though nodding to himself, and sets off to follow him, slowly, paying attention to where he goes, whom he speaks with. Via

Parioli, Via Monteolo, downhill. Zoboli seems to be relaxed, like someone who is walking with no particular purpose, in no rush, looking around now and then, but not often really, just enough to check the traffic at a crossroads, or in front of a shop window, and without ever turning around, without ever realizing he is being followed. Maybe he is going into town to do the shopping? Then suddenly he stops and Ferrero finds himself too close, but Zoboli goes into a telephone box (strange, so close to home; doesn't he have his mobile with him?), and so Ferrero turns to look at a shop window, swallowing as he does so. Why is he so anxious that his guts are in turmoil, his throat is tightening? It is not as though he has to speak, to say anything, after all. All he has to do for now is watch.

Then Zoboli reappears, a look of concentration on his face, pausing as with one hand he eases the doors closed, stopping them from slamming. He is red in the face, but maybe it's the heat, or maybe that's just the impression Ferrero gets, who knows, because it is not as though you can be sure about colours or details from thirty metres away. And anyway it is nothing more than an instant as Zoboli turns and starts walking, slightly agitated now, irritated, perhaps because of the phone call. That makes life easier for me, Ferrero thinks. If he is preoccupied with other things, more important things, then I can get closer to him. Twenty metres will be alright, no closer than that, but at that distance it would be easy to take him out... no more than he deserves and then it would all be over. Instinctively he puts his hand into his jacket pocket, the one on the right-hand side with the bulge, as though he is about to pull something out without thinking, but then he stops, saying to himself that he's not here just for this. And by this time anyway a woman has stopped Zoboli.

There is nothing going on between them, Ferrero thinks almost immediately, nothing personal, nothing he would be interested in. An ordinary sort of woman, almost elderly, with dyed hair. He sees that she is insisting about something, touching Zoboli's arm, but he is shaking his head, politely, with a smile that carries just a touch of intolerance. Can't blame him, he thinks. In the past he would often run out of patience when dealing with the pushiness of some old folks. Just how much do we have to put up with in one single day? And just what consequences are there in a delayed explosion of anger, in bottling up a sort of resentment? He knows about all this only too well. And not just one day's worth. Eighteen years' worth.

After a while she gives up as he smiles, reassuringly, and goes off waving, some distance between them, like friends. He is clearly heading towards the centre now: Via Repubblica, Via Roma, and then he is at the K2 bar, the one in Piazza Marconi, with the tables outside – the wicker chairs, the white napkins. As soon as he sits down a waiter approaches. Zoboli smiles (knowingly?) and the waiter goes away immediately. Ferrero takes a seat three tables behind him, near the road, and worries rather illogically that the same waiter might come to his table, or that the man from the Bandieri, the only person in town he has spoken to, might spot him. But neither of these things happens. He orders a beer, even though he has already had one and he would like an ice-cream, but the beer is better because it can be drunk quickly and he might have to get up suddenly to follow Zoboli. That could happen.

But it does not. The afternoon is slipping by slowly, in the slightly less muggy heat of the shady square, with Zoboli still sitting there and every now and then looking at his watch and sighing, more resigned than tense as time goes by. Then he gets up to pay and leaves, slightly distracted, and it is clear he is going back home because he takes the same route, without stopping. This time he crosses no one's path, not even a chance meeting. In the garden, before entering the house, he puts the car in the garage. Not the Seicento, the other one. Ferrero just needs a glance as he slows down in front of the gate, to see it as it crunches through the gravel. A Volvo S40, 1600 cc, registration AV993WD. Brand new.

It is three in the morning. She is fast asleep in the double bed, her face turned towards the open door. But he is awake. He had been asleep until half an hour ago, and now he is lying there, thinking, without falling back into sleep. He would like a cigarette, but he would have to get up and open a drawer and he is afraid of making a noise, of waking her from her sleep; her breath is deep, her lips slightly open. It is best she sleeps, definitely. It was best she did not wait up for him while he was downstairs trying to write for tomorrow's appointment. It was best she did not ask him to make love. He is not sleepy at all now and that is why the ringing telephone on the bedside table does not make him jump.

There is no voice. Just a slightly hoarse breathing, like someone with a throat full of catarrh. He waits a second, without saying hello or anything else, in the hope that whoever it is might reveal themselves, might say something, if they want to. Then the metallic click of the phone being hung up.

Who could that have been? thinks Zoboli. There are idiots and perverts all over the place. All that matters is that whoever it was does not try again because they might wake her. Indeed, after just a second or two:

'Who was it?'

'No one, Miriam. A wrong number. Go back to sleep.'

Breakfast together the following morning: peaceful, pleasantly uncomplicated. Two small pizzas warmed up in the oven for him, a yoghurt for her, and then an espresso coffee with that thin layer of foam on the top, just as they both like it. And then the desire to chat a little, to tell each other a few things. He has his appointment, she has to tidy up and do some shopping, before going to Modena in the afternoon. They will see each other at lunchtime, otherwise they will speak on the phone. Just as they did once upon a time, at the beginning, when they were just married and any news, no matter how small, drove them to search each other out. Then the years had gone by – habit and fatigue had entered the equation. Children had not come, but that is not what it was, no. Childlessness unites people even more, sometimes, or at least they knew others for whom this was true. It was more the feelings that had changed them. Because people change as life unfolds, inside and outside, and no one remains the same and you cannot stop time. And then someone else comes along and something inside you is born again, burns again. It is all to do with feelings, yes. They do not make you any happier, but they make you feel more alive. And it's worth it, even if they sometimes make you suffer.

'Something wrong?'

There is a strange look on her face as she asks him, and perhaps it is even sweetness that is in her eyes. He smiles and shakes his head, without speaking, and thinks instead that at this moment, to an outsider they would look like two people made to complement each other, to alleviate with quiet, thoughtful affection their respective incompleteness.

Outside, they say goodbye after taking the cars out of the garage and opening the gate. Together they take a look at the mail box, on the right. Leaflets, as usual, she thinks... they have even started distributing them in the evenings.

'Giulio, take a look at this...'

Behind a supermarket flyer, there is a folded photocopy, as big as a page from a broadsheet newspaper. They stare at it together for a few seconds as she opens it up with both hands; he is standing behind her, looking over her shoulder. *Il Resto del Carlino*, NEWS FROM MODENA, runs across the top of the page. And then there is a big six-column headline, alongside the obituaries.

'What is this?'

But he has already taken it from her hands and is now moving towards the Volvo, almost running and he gets in and closes the door still holding that piece of paper and then he is off, at speed, leaving her there at the gate. Without giving her even the time to speak, time to think. Without giving anything away.

But she had read something. 'Last night: accident or crime?' And then the date: 23 February 1980. Eighteen years ago.

CHAPTER THREE

The appointment

The 'Athos Lodi' Foundation, set up to encourage philo-
sophical and literary research, has been based for years in
the centre of Guiglia, in the convent in Via Di Vittorio. The
Foundation's wealth, which according to local gossip is con-
siderable, has always been managed by the board of direc-
tors of the Banco di San Geminiano e San Prospero, ever
since the creation of the Foundation, when the current president deposited it all in the bank's coffers. The president
gave the institution his own name: Don Athos Lodi, fifty-
five years of age, priest and former high-school history and
philosophy teacher, author of many papers published in academic journals, spends his time between Guiglia and
Modena where he owns and runs a small publishing house.
And it is this publishing house, Mutina, that has taken on
the task of publishing the proceedings of the national conference on 'Formiggini and Early Twentieth-century
Publishing', to be held in Modena in October. Prestigious
contributions are expected from some of the grand old men
of academia – Garin, Roncaglia, Ramondini. Don Lodi and
Ramondini are both due to present papers.

Standing in the middle of the room, Don Lodi looks out of
the windows at the green garden, paying no attention to his
pretty young secretary who is sitting behind him.
Ramondini is already here and has placed a notebook (his
own, this time) on the table, but he has not opened it yet
and is silent, simply looking at the books that surround
them. Oak bookcases decorated with inlay cover three walls

from floor to ceiling. The books are also antique and their spines are almost all of the same colour, all having been bound so that a uniform, ivory tint pervades the room. No one says a word, not even Ramondini who opens his mouth two or three times as though undecided, staring at the other man's back rather than at the girl's crossed legs, until the door opens and Zoboli walks in, red in the face.

'Am I late?'

'We can start immediately,' says Don Lodi, without answering the question. He points to a leather armchair for Zoboli, on the other side of the table, and he himself sits. With brisk decision, he comes straight to the point: 'I've heard there's some problem between you, some sort of conflict. I don't want to know any more than that. All I want to say is that it mustn't influence the conference. That is to say, our work.' Zoboli and Ramondini look each other in the eye, then turn to the priest without speaking. The secretary stops, her fountain pen still raised, and she too looks at the priest quizzically, as though asking whether she should start taking minutes or not; then she decides she should not and lingers over the preliminaries, repeating to herself what she is writing: 'Today, Tuesday 23 June 1998, in the Foundation's offices, a preliminary meeting takes place...'

'Let's just make that clear, first off. Because the conference is an important opportunity, for us and for the Foundation. To let people know about us, to add value to our research... to our results. To show people that out here in the provinces there's good work being done, that we know how to work together...'

He is speaking with authority, Ramondini thinks to himself, with a bit of vanity too, the vanity he has always been aware of, even from their high-school days, the vanity that had first made him curious and then had charmed him. Because Don Lodi was an attractive man, despite the slightly ascetic austerity of his intense gaze, behind those glasses and the vaguely derisory disdain expressed in his eyebrows. But once you got to know him, out of school, there was not much pretence about him, he really was like that. With his one metre eighty height, his great learning, his capacity for encouragement and decision, he exuded energy and authority. Then there were the corners of his mouth, curving slightly upwards, that sometimes formed an unexpected smile, a sign of liveliness, or a sudden gaiety, but indicating an ever-present inner serenity.

'The second thing, on the other hand, is that I'm a bit worried. And I'd like you two to reassure me now. What I mean is...' and he clears his throat, but not because he has a cough, 'just three months before the conference it seems we still have no significant discoveries to report from our research... therefore we don't even have a definite line. Or am I wrong? So, over the next few days let's get some good ideas sorted out, otherwise all we'll have to present at the conference will be our embarrassed smiles.'

He has spoken for everyone, but he is not referring to himself, that is quite clear. Because all three, as they turn to him, perceive that half smile, that faith in himself, in his own intelligence.

Ramondini finally speaks, 'You're being unfair in saying that. We've worked hard and we haven't finished yet...'

'I know that. By the way, which of you two is going to present the paper?'

'Me.' And Ramondini's ears suddenly turn red while Zoboli opens his mouth as though he is about to speak, but then he changes his mind and looks at the floor, at a strip of sunlight on the tiles.

'Good. Come on then. Tell me about your discoveries, and then I'll tell you about what I've been doing. That way we won't cover the same ground...'

'Or contradict ourselves...'

'Precisely. Come on, let's hear it.'

Calmly, the professor reads a summary, prepared beforehand, of all the material gathered by Zoboli. It is an accurate, precise summary, almost as though the work were actually his. The priest in the meantime chooses a cigar and lights it, slowly, an almost ritual gesture, then he assumes a comfortable position, leaning slightly backwards, his elbows planted firmly on the armrests, every now and then looking at the slowly lengthening ash on the cigar. In the end he says nothing but remains in that posture, concentrating, until a movement of his head makes the ash fall.

Then Ramondini says, 'Can I ask you a question?'

'Go ahead.'

'Why are you so interested in this research?'

'Not this research in particular, but all the research I do and then publish. I've always said so, no? There are two great loves in my life...' and he smiles, '... the Foundation and the publishing house. Publishing things you've discovered yourself, or even things someone else has discovered, means disseminating culture, truth. It means tying your name, your passions, to something that remains, however few or many may ever read it...'

'A true *raison d'être*,' murmurs Zoboli under his breath.

'That's it!' The priest looks at him, nodding. 'And even more than that. It's an educational, a moral vocation. Or do you think we can use the word vocation only in religious terms? No, scholars too, publishers... men of culture, like

25

me, like you... we have the courage of a vocation, of a calling. And it's not a written manifesto, it's an inner manifesto: you do this because you can't do anything else...' He looks them all in the eye, slowly, even the secretary who does not understand, who has a puzzled expression, almost as though asking him to repeat. Then he smiles again.

'Don't worry, Simona. You can take the rest of the day off. You can finish the minutes some other time, if you manage to make sense of what I've just said.'

The girl blushes and silently swallows some air. The minutes slip from her hands and she bends down, rigidly, to pick them up before standing up again and heading for the door with a rather pathetic display of seriousness. Don Lodi picks up where he had left off as if nothing has happened.

'At school I talked to you a lot about the soul. Do you remember? Well, today if you lose your soul, you lose your dignity, your freedom. And we lose our soul when we relinquish our dreams, our ideals... when we give up on what we feel we've been born to do. Out of fear of punishment, for example.' His voice cracks for an instant and becomes a whisper. 'Or out of guilt.'

'I'm not sure I understand.'

'It's not important, Luigi. I was speaking more for myself than for you. What I mean is that we have to live for something, always, and I have always lived for this. For writing, publishing something of myself and my work.' He stares at them again and his voice becomes certain. 'Because life is a slow-acting poison – it eats away at sense, it makes us submit to everything. The only true compensation is work for its own sake.'

'But you don't always find what you're looking for in work...'

He smiles. 'I know, Giulio. But we mustn't give up just for that reason. We are all what we are looking for. And to be content with finding instead of looking for something is a true betrayal of all faith.' He stands up, opens a drawer and takes out a sheet of paper. 'But enough of that. Now it's my turn to tell you what I've discovered.'

Out in the road, in the rich light of eleven o'clock in the morning, Zoboli walks unhappily, nervously. And it is not the meeting, that is not the problem. He will forget the meeting in two or three days' time, he knows that well. His disquiet comes from another source, and it will not leave him alone, it kept him from concentrating just now, to the extent that he only uttered one or two sentences during the meeting and he wonders if the others realized. He walks head down towards his Volvo, following the thread of his thoughts, then he lifts his head and sees it immediately. White, placed sideways under the wiper on the windscreen. A sheet of paper just like the one they found two hours earlier: he does not even need to read it. So he folds it and puts it in his pocket. He already knows what to do with it, of course, and he knows he will not show it to Miriam; she might get frightened, or she might want to help him, and that is the last thing he wants. He looks around slowly as he opens the door, but there is no one watching him, nothing unusual at all, and in truth he really did not think there would be. But now he begins to understand.

'What's going on, Giulio?'

'Nothing... why?'

'I'm talking about this morning. Look at me – do you think I'm stupid? You saw that sheet of paper and you ran off, for no reason. Or rather, only you know the reason...'

'It's nothing. Nothing at all. It's just... I'm tired, that's what it is. I get upset over nothing...' Both upset and sad, he looks at her, knowing she will not believe him. 'It's just a difficult time... it won't last. Once the conference is over, the stress will disappear... and then we'll go away, take a trip somewhere... we've been talking about it for a while, haven't we? Believe me, it'll all be over soon. Just try to be patient...'

He would like to ask her to stand by him, but he cannot do it.

'It's not the conference, Giulio. It's not just that.'

'You don't believe me?'

'I'd like to, but there's that photocopy.'

'Come on. It's a joke... just a stupid joke.'

'If you really thought that, then you wouldn't have reacted like that. You do realize that, don't you?'

He lowers his head because he doesn't know what to say, and only now does she take his hand.

'Don't you want me to help you?'

He pulls himself together, but his voice changes, 'No. It's not a good idea.'

'Not even to talk about it?'

'No, there's no need.' He shakes his head. 'And I have to go out now.'

'But you haven't even finished eating...'

'It doesn't matter. I'm not hungry now.'

'Change your shirt at least. You're all sweaty.'

He is uncertain as he stands there in the entrance, car keys in his hand. Then he decides.

'Yes, thanks.'

'There's one already ironed on the bed. So, will you be back before I go?'

From the bedroom comes the quiet reply together with the

sound of a drawer being opened.

'I don't know, it depends...'

'Professor...'

Sweating profusely in the sunshine, the owner of the Hotel Bandieri seems even fatter than usual without his counter to contain him within the space against the wall.

'Excuse me, but I wanted to tell you something. There's a stranger in the hotel who's been asking about you...'

'About me?'

'Yes. A man called Ferrero, from Turin. Do you know him?'

'No... I don't think so.' He stares into space, trying to remember, but it is obvious he is slightly troubled. 'No, I really don't think I do.'

'I thought as much.'

'Why?'

'Because there's something suspicious about him, something not right. Not that he's done anything, he's only asked about you. But...'

'Just a minute. What's he like?'

'He certainly wouldn't go unnoticed.' He stares at Zoboli with a conspiratorial air: 'A handsome man, about forty. Tall, thin, green eyes and a moustache. He goes around wearing a jacket and tie in this heat...'

'Are you sure he's from Turin?'

'Dead sure. His accent's a total giveaway. And there's another thing that sticks out.'

'What's that?'

'He's as pale as a corpse. As though he's just come out of prison.' And the fat man laughs, tickled by his own thought. But now Zoboli is even more troubled.

*

There is a dark blue Mercedes sitting at the beginning of Via del Cavallo. It is a 280S, almost twenty years old, but it is still a fine car, and a few people have given it a second look as they passed, because you do not see many of them nowadays. And Zoboli is on the other side of the road, a cigarette in his mouth, lost in memories, uncertain whether to go the Bandieri to see for himself. Then he finally notices the car, with a man sitting inside, a man who may be looking straight at him. He is wearing sunglasses, that's why he cannot be sure where he is looking, but he is sure he has never seen him before, has no idea who he is.

But the car is familiar. And suddenly the worry rises, it catches his breath, dries up his mouth, and he tries to think it through, to keep the anxiety under control. And he says to himself it's impossible, it can't be true. Because the past is frightening, the past that everyone carries around inside, the past that no one goes looking for unless they are forced to. Forced by someone or by life. Is this what is happening now?

So he decides. He crosses the road, but the man casually, almost as though he has not even seen him, starts the engine and drives off. The car moves out of sight round the corner, but Zoboli stands there for a long time, looking, his eyes staring ahead, as though the car is actually moving along a long, straight road and he can still see it gradually disappearing. In the end he snaps out of his thoughts and goes into a telephone booth.

In the bedroom Miriam is packing a bag, preparing to drive the Seicento to Modena, where she will spend the night. She makes this trip once a week in summer, it is a routine now.

She collects the post, checks the house, waters the plants. She goes through her mental list of the few necessary things: toothpaste, toothbrush, pyjamas... pyjamas, yes, best take those new cotton ones, they are at the bottom of the drawer. And by instinct, through that lucky train of thought that sometimes just happens to us, she thinks of another drawer, her husband's this time, the bottom one in the chest of drawers, the one that has something particular at the bottom of it. But it is not a pair of pyjamas. It is something that is not here now, and yet she is rooting thoroughly, on her knees, red in the face, searching through the whole thing. She goes through Giulio's underwear – pants, socks, vests – right to the bottom. That is where he keeps it, the pistol, he had even shown it to her – for legitimate self defence he had said. He could have taken it some time ago, she mutters, almost as though trying to convince herself that it is not important... or he could have taken it an hour ago, when he changed his shirt. And in that case... suddenly she feels worried and wishes he were back home already so that she could look into his eyes, ask him so many things. But she knows, deep down, that this will not be possible. He will not be back soon. She finishes packing, the tension within her still high.

At the Bandieri Ferrero goes up the stairs, almost running, frowning. With the key already in the door he does not notice the woman who has come out of another room and is standing behind him in the half-light of the corridor. When he turns he sees her there, motionless, and all he can really make out is the light colour of her face, her almost naked breasts and the red of her mouth. He understands immediately. 'No thanks,' he says quickly, in a whisper, mumbling the words. Then, still motionless behind him as he turns the key in the lock, she says in a strange, almost cruel voice, 'Sure you're not... ?' And she lifts two fingers to her earlobe, in the classic Italian suggestion that he is gay. He smiles, unperturbed, and shakes his head. 'No, it's not that. I'm just in a hurry.'

He locks himself in, pulls something out of his right-hand pocket and wraps it in a towel, which he then hides at the bottom of his wardrobe. Then he takes a leather-bound notebook from his bag and leaves again, moving rapidly. All this takes no longer than a minute.

'Sorry to bother you. My name is Alberto Ferrero...'

He had rung the bell twice before getting an answer and now an unfriendly Zoboli is looking at him through the half-open door.

'... and it was Professor Mattioli at the University of Turin who gave me your name.'

'With regard to?'

'With regard to Antonio Delfini. He's read your book. In fact, I've read it too...'

'I see,' Zoboli says, nodding approvingly. 'Are you working on Delfini too?'

'Yes, that's right,' and he smiles. 'I'm writing a monograph, for the Professor... a small introductory book, but I'm looking for some advice...'

'Yes?'

'Well, I read in a note in your book that there's a Delfini collection, or something of that kind, at the Estense Library in Modena, and since I don't have access to it and you've already studied it...'

'You'd like some information.' And Zoboli's tone is now

more relaxed, almost understanding. 'I see, yes. But in the end you'll still have to visit yourself, if you want to study the manuscripts critically.'

'Yes, of course. But for now I'd just like some preliminaries, pointers in the right direction. To save time. What I mean is, are there unpublished letters, or plans for narrative works, ideas? Or perhaps even complete unpublished works, things that haven't even appeared in journals...'

'I can tell you all about that. We just have to look at my notes.'

'Thank you... and apropos of journals, if there are any little-known magazines that published anything, maybe something Delfini published later, even years later, with textual differences. You know... variants and all that...'

'That's a trickier matter. Or it's more difficult to say from memory. Let me think...'

'Obviously later on I'll have to take a look at these things personally, even if it's just to transcribe them... any significant texts...'

'Of course, of course,' and Zoboli looks over the other man's shoulders as he starts thinking. 'Well, let's do this... are you just passing through? Or are you here for a few days?'

'For a few days. I'm on holiday.'

'And where are you staying?'

'Here in Guiglia, at the Hotel Bandieri.'

'Good. Very good. I thought you'd perhaps come out from Modena...'

'I've been to Modena. That's how I discovered you were here.'

'Let's do this then,' Zoboli is convinced now. 'Come back this evening.' He looks at his watch, thinks for a moment.

'Let's say, yes, nine thirty. In the meantime I'll pull out all the notes I took for my book. We'll see if they're of any use.' He stares as a doubt comes to him. 'Is that alright?'

'That's fine by me. I just don't want to be any bother...'

'No trouble, believe me. My wife's away until tomorrow and I'm here on my own. We'll have all the time we need.' And he smiles now, for the first time, as they shake hands. 'It was high time someone from outside Modena paid some attention to Delfini. In truth I'd already tried in Turin, with Einaudi, for his diaries, but nothing ever came of it...'

Zoboli's expression is serious now as through the window he watches Ferrero leave. He picks up the telephone and dials the number from memory: 'He's just been here.' His tone is decided, curt. 'It's him, there's no doubt about it. He's thinner, he's grown a moustache, but it's him alright. I told you before...'

The other voice says something. It's a question.

'What do you mean, what shall we do? We're in this together, don't forget. Come here this evening... yes, to my house, just before nine. No, Miriam's not here, she's gone... we have to sort it all out, and we'll do it together.'

He hangs up, then lets out a long, slow sigh. Even if he does not really believe it, he feels some lightening of the tension now. Because this is the end of the deceit, of the doubt. No more hypotheses, conjectures: now there is some certainty. That is why he is not anxious when the phone rings. He is just a bit irritated. Perhaps the other man does not understand, perhaps he is scared.

'Hello. How are you?'

On the other end of the line, unmistakable, that French 'r'. And her voice, the same as always, just like a little girl's.

'Ah... it's you. Fine.'

'Are you busy?'

'No, not at all.'

'Because I can call back later if that would be better.'

'No, no, really. Go ahead.' But he says nothing else, as though preoccupied. And she picks up on this fact.

'Are you angry?'

'Why should I be angry?'

'Because of yesterday afternoon. I couldn't make it, I really couldn't. I said yes on the phone, but then...'

'I know. Or rather I imagined so. I waited for you...'

'Did you wait long?'

'Quite a long time. But it doesn't matter. There's no need to talk about it.'

He wonders if she has taken the earring from her right earlobe. She always does that when she is on the phone.

'I'm sorry...'

'It doesn't matter, I said. Water under the bridge.'

'Shall I come over tonight?'

He smiles and in the earpiece he can hear his own breath.

'I could make amends...' she adds.

But now he is alarmed and his voice gives this away, 'Tonight? No, we can't...'

'Why not? Miriam's away, I know. Carlo's away too... it wouldn't be the first time, would it? Or is it just that you don't feel like it?'

God, what a pain. 'No, that's not it. I can't this time...'

'Why?'

'Because someone's coming. Work... after supper... the university.' He's spoken rapidly, coldly, hoping she will not insist, hoping she might be offended, that she will not ask any more questions.

'If it's like that...'

35

'I'll call you tomorrow, okay?'

'No, that's no good.'

'Why?'

'Because Miriam will be here tomorrow.'

'But there are plenty of places we could go. Not just here, my house. That's assuming you can make it...'

'If I can't, that makes us even.'

'Sort of... come on, we're not kids. It's not out of spite. If I say I can't, I can't. It's a job, if it doesn't work out then I'm in trouble.' He takes a breath and adds, 'We'll have other chances...'

'Oh, of course... bye then.'

'I'll call you, alright?'

But she has already hung up, and now she is there in the entrance, sitting on the bench, hands on her knees, trying to think. But she soon gives up. Because understanding is not easy, and it is not easy chasing away the disappointment, the suspicion. The only thing to do, to rid herself of all her doubts, would be to go and see with her own eyes. Yes, she'll think about that, she says to herself. Perhaps she really will go, perhaps she will not be brave enough. But she is already more composed now as she puts her earring back on and looks at her watch to see how long it will be before darkness falls.

CHAPTER FOUR

A dead man

At nine o'clock on Wednesday morning the Seicento pulls up at the end of Via Dante Alighieri. The woman who gets out leaves the engine running, unlocks the gates and opens them wide before getting back into the car, putting it into first gear and driving in over the crunching gravel. No sign of the Volvo, but she is not worried, it will be in the garage. He must be at home because he has finished that research work in Modena, at the Estense Library. Only now does she notice that the shutters are still closed, and she smiles. Perhaps he is still asleep.

She turns off the engine, goes and closes the gate, then calmly turns round, leaving the car unlocked. She does not even consider ringing the bell, not wanting to wake him. The door is closed, of course, and she takes the house keys from her bag. But the door is not properly locked, it has only been pulled shut: that means he is certainly at home. Now she is uncertain whether to call out, to tell him she is back.

But there is something not right. It is all too quiet. Only the insistent ticking of the pendulum from the clock in the entrance disturbs the stillness of the silence. The air is cold and carries no smell apart from the perfume of the flowers – there are lots of them in a vase on the shelf below the mirror, but suddenly she feels they give off a feeling of sadness. She chases that thought away – an absurdity – as she walks into the living room, waiting to hear a step, a voice.

'Giulio?'

She decided to call out, in the end, but the voice she hears in the half-light sounds strange, different. It seems hoarse, tinged with a slight thread of worry. She switches on the light and crosses the room, looking around, but there is nothing to see – all is silent, clean, just like yesterday. Now she ought to go up the stairs towards the rooms above, but something stops her – the light is on in her husband's study, shining through the smoked glass. It is odd that he has left it on all night. And, standing there in front of the door, she wonders why; she decides to knock, almost out of shyness.

No voice from within. She waits a moment, then turns the handle, feeling it cold in her sweating hand and then sees the filmy marks made by her fingers, sees them evaporate immediately when she lets go. Nothing, not even a rustle. Then, with a strange sense of embarrassment, she opens the door wide – and she sees him.

He sits slumped forward on the chair, his head lying on the desk. The blood – my God! so much of it! – dirtied every-thing before it clotted and it has even dripped onto the floor. There is a hole in his right temple, she can see it clearly from where she stands, and as she looks she discovers in an instant a new impotence – an incapacity to feel compassion for something that both attracts and horrifies her and she wonders what his face must look like now, pressed as it is against the desktop.

As she swallows, suppressing her nausea, she becomes aware, surprised, at how lucid she is. Her eyes are wide open, taking in all the details in this room with the light on, in this absurd quietness. The pistol is there, on the desk, just to the right of his head. Instinct moves her closer, to get a better look, she has the strength for that, and it looks like his gun... but it is too hot in here with the black, folded silhou-ette of the body that now seems to bloat in the silence, filling all the available space with its presence. She wants to leave now – she has seen enough and she believes she is actually moving, swaying uncertainly towards the threshold. But she continues to look. The pistol is there, shiny, just inches from his head. And his squashed face, which she cannot see. She wonders what it must look like, she cannot help but wonder. But not now.

The police car arrives without sirens blaring, and when Miriam opens the door there are two of them. 'Inspector Cataldo,' says the first one, in civilian clothes and holding out his badge: a tall man, clean-shaven, more or less her own age. The other is his deputy, Muliere: evidently older, with a deep voice and a thick moustache that contrasts with his rather feminine surname. Then the others start arriving: first a doctor, then two policemen in civilian clothes – Cataldo has never seen them before. Then a photographer, a ballistics expert and a fingerprint technician. They are all whispering busily around the corpse.

Muliere stands to the right of the desk and frowns as he looks at the body, then he leans slightly forward, smells the skin on Zoboli's arm and looks at Cataldo, who nods. The Inspector stands on the other side of the desk, hands on hips, as he too studies the dead man, screwing his eyes up, his jaw stiff, as though hoping – through the intensity of his gaze – to penetrate the mystery of this death, heedless of the quiet buzzing behind him. The study is full of people now, but no one gets in anyone else's way, no toes are stepped upon. Everyone moves confidently and discreetly, demonstrating professionalism and respect in the presence of death. And their hands – swift, efficient, slipped into rubber gloves as thin as condoms – hands that pick up the pistol, touching it with only the tips of fingers, placing it delicately in a plastic bag, as soon as the photos and the measurements are complete. Other hands are busy working under the desk, with magnifying glass and tweezers, searching for something, perhaps strands of hair. The fingerprint technician too, with his brushes, moves silently from the handle to the lock, from the desktop to the floor, spreading a veil of silver-grey dust over the surfaces. The same as always, thinks Cataldo... here we go again.

'Here's the shell.'

The ballistics expert lifts his head up slowly and looks at Cataldo with his short-sighted eyes. He is evidently satisfied and he is a trifle clumsy in his movements as he stands up, but then he talks calmly and precisely.

'Calibre 7.65 bullet. Automatic pistol.' He nods towards the plastic bag on the desk. 'That one.' But he picks up on a silent reproof in the eyes of the other man, and adds immediately, 'Of course, we'll have to run a ballistics test, but if you want my opinion right now...'

'It doesn't matter,' says Cataldo, thanking him with a gesture. 'That'll do for the moment.'

Because it is Speedy Gonzales he is interested in now: with his white linen suit, his bald patch illuminated by the sun. Dr Arletti is his name and he is already at work, grumbling now and then to himself, with all the methodical impassivity of someone who has grown old denying himself emotions like compassion and embarrassment. Not that he is the best of the medical examiners, but he is certainly the quickest in coming up with a diagnosis. And this doesn't seem to be a difficult case.

The first thing he does is to study Zoboli's face close up, indifferently, looking for traces of gunpowder, and now he is studying the bullet hole in the temple and the ragged wound at the back of the head. After this, with a grunt, he moves the dead man's arm, bending the fingers and pushing the head to one side to check for rigor mortis. Then he returns to examine the arms and hands, opening them to study the palms. Then he straightens up, rubbing his own hands with an immaculate handkerchief, and gets ready to speak, aware of the fact that everyone is waiting.

'Entry through the right temple. Straight line of fire. Exit through the left occipital region, at the base of the skull. You've found the shell, right? Good. The bullet went straight through the skull and he died instantly. Time of death...' and he coughs now, mechanically, '... well, I'd say twelve hours ago, perhaps even a bit more. But we'll have to wait for the post-mortem.'

A few people nod, no one speaks. Except for Cataldo, when Arletti has put his instruments back in their black case.

'I'd like the post-mortem by this evening. Is that possible?'

'Alright.' And he closes his bag with a click, without objecting. 'But have him taken to the mortuary as soon as you can.'

Cataldo says thank you, then opens the door for him. In the living room he sees the widow, Miriam, he remembers, sitting, staring at the people who are leaving. For a moment their eyes meet, just the time it takes to close the door, time enough for him to carry away an image in his mind. A slender, elegant woman of about forty: a grey silk blouse worn with a black skirt, high-heeled shoes with ankle straps, dark hair in a page-boy cut. Probably a strong, independent woman. But she has been crying. The unmistakable signs are there – the red eyes, the swollen face.

He turns to look at the room, his shoulders against the

door. Everything is normal, or so it seems. Zoboli obviously fell forward after he was shot, but not very far because the chair is a bit low, the desk is high and his arms supported him. Right. Just as it is right that there is all that blood, despite the small blackened hole, blackened with coagulated blood, at his temple. There is a big dark stain on the rug behind the chair, and blood on the tiles, a lot of it. And it is on the chair too, on one edge of the desk and even at some distance from the corpse – drops of thickened, dark blood. Perhaps he is imagining the sweet smell of it, a smell he knows well and for a moment he wants to open the window, but then he thinks of the temperature, which should be kept constant, and the flies. There is one already there, on the wall, and it seems motionless, but on closer inspection it is rubbing its legs before flying off to come to rest elsewhere, buzzing in satisfaction. 'The flies have a great time of it with the shit, the heat and the blood.' The voice shakes him – Muliere is standing there in front of the window.

'Petronio's on his way, Inspector...'

And the tone of voice suggests, good luck to you.

'So what's the situation, exactly, Inspector?' The Investigating Magistrate coughs his question, a nervous cough that has become a habit. 'Why have I only received a superficial breakdown of the facts?'

As if by contagion, Cataldo clears his throat too.

'There's very little to say, for now. We were informed this morning, about nine thirty. His wife phoned.' Instinctively he gestures towards her, as though she were actually there with them. 'I mean, the widow...'

'Suicide?'

'Looks like it...'

'I only ask because I bumped into Arletti just now out front and he's sure, even before doing the post-mortem. Especially because of the edge of the halo, something you can see with the naked eye... you know what I mean?'

Of course he knows. Grazed and bruised edge it says in the manual: a shot fired at point-blank range, the gunpowder penetrates the skin and leaves this kind of halo all around the entry hole of the bullet...

'That's it. He's sure. For him it's one hundred percent a suicide.'

But Cataldo says nothing. He looks at Petronio, a very tall man with a child's face, greying hair, glasses like a top-of-the-class student, who in the meantime stares, perhaps taken aback by Cataldo's reticence.

'But what do you think?'

'I think it's a bit early to say. Of course, it's possible. It's just that...'

'Just that?...'

'No note. No letter... nothing.' He stares back. 'Usually they do something like that.'

'But that's no proof.'

'I know.' But neither is the edge of the halo, he thinks, but he does not say it. Because it is possible to point a gun at another man's temple and to produce the same result. As long as the dead man trusted you, did not expect it...

'Was the Beretta his?'

'I don't know yet. I've just started. Just like you.'

'Right.'

'But I think so. I'll bet it's his and I bet it's registered.'

He is not hoping it is true. Neither of them hope that. Petronio nods, then asks: 'And what are you going to do now?'

'Nothing. It's up to forensics now. Lab tests,' he sighs. 'The usual thing... it's not up to me.'

And since Petronio says nothing:

'The fingerprints on the pistol, the paraffin nitrate test on the corpse, the microscope analysis on the bullet and the barrel... all I can do is talk to the widow.'

'I saw her out there...'

'To get an idea of a possible motive. For now.'

He walks outside with him, out of respect. He shakes his hand. In the garden outside the house two undertakers from the Council are waiting with a green zippered body bag, just like in the movies.

'Signora Zoboli...'

Who knows what type of life pulses behind those questioning eyes. He always wonders that... every time. 'I need to talk to you.'

She seems surprised and looks at him without saying anything. She runs a hand over her mouth. Then she moves to one side, letting Cataldo pass between herself and the table in the living room, her eyes fixed on his back.

'My heartfelt condolences... and I wouldn't trouble you if it weren't important. Believe me.' He speaks softly, sympathetically, with that smile, the sad one he has used on too many occasions. 'But I have to ask one or two questions. To try to understand. It's my job.'

She closes her eyes for a moment. Then she makes a slow gesture in the air with her hand.

'Please. After all, as you've said – it's your job.'

'Thank you. So, first off... what did your husband do?'

'He was doing some research at the university...'

'So... a lot of hope or expectation, very little salary. Is that right?'

'Yes.'

'And what did he live on... if I may?'

'Supply jobs now and then at school... here and there... wherever. And then he was independently wealthy... he got by.'

'I understand. And he'd never thought of a change?'

'What do you mean?'

'To this situation. To look for a permanent job.'

'No. Firstly because he liked it, he lived for his research. And then because he was preparing a paper for a national conference and this... how shall I put it? This would have given him a lot of credit. It would have helped him in the next *concorso*. At least that's what he said...'

'Alright. So you don't know of any economic worries – business or anything like that – that were weighing on his mind?'

'No, nothing.'

'And lately, think carefully about this, your husband's behaviour, his actions... had anything made you suspect that he was worried, I mean... that something might happen to him?'

'No.' But she lowers her eyes. Trying to remember something? In any case, Cataldo gives her time. 'No, I told you. There's been nothing strange.'

'Do you know of anyone,' he starts again, 'who might hold a grudge against him?'

'No one, as far as I know.'

'Is it possible, I'm sorry to suggest this, that he shot himself in a moment of depression?'

The question comes at a moment when she has pulled out a handkerchief to dry her eyes, but she shakes her head suddenly and almost shouts, 'No! Not that!' Then she presses the handkerchief against her mouth and starts crying.

'Why?'

'Because he was full of life, he loved life... and then the strength to keep going comes when you know that there's someone who wants you. And I was there for him, he knew that.'

'Sometimes it's not enough,' says Cataldo, looking at her almost kindly. 'If you're up against something evil, an enemy...'

'He would have defended himself against an enemy. He would never have run away... he didn't want to run away from anything. Do that once, and you do it for ever, he used to say... it means running away from life.' She swallows, gets her breath back. 'It takes courage. Grit your teeth, summon all the strength in your soul...'

'Are those his words?' asks Cataldo, thinking the phrase has a good ring to it.

'Yes. He said that once.'

And now he has to ask her another question, before their conversation shifts elsewhere: 'Why did you say just now that he would have defended himself?'

She is motionless now. Her eyes fixed straight ahead. There is a strange tranquillity in her. Then her mouth moves into a grimace. It is as though she is about to sob, but nothing comes. Her voice is dull when she says:

'There's something I have to tell you.'

'I'm listening.'

'The pistol, the one on the desk.'

'Was it his?'

'Yes. He took it from the drawer, where it's always been kept. I'm sure about that.'

'So he was frightened by something. Or he wanted to

defend himself... but from who?'

'From a newspaper article,' she suddenly whispers, as though trying to grasp at some detail in a thick fog or in a dream. Cataldo looks at her in puzzlement before she continues:

'It was in the mailbox, a photocopy, yesterday morning. It must have been put there during the night.'

'And can you remember anything about it? The headline, the date?'

'No, just the newspaper. It was the *Resto del Carlino*, from years ago. I could tell by the graphics.' And she adds, by way of explanation, 'We've been buying it regularly, for many years...'

'You're sure?'

She nods.

'It's not much to go on.' And after a second, 'You really can't remember anything else?'

'No. Because he grabbed it out of my hand straight away.'

'Ah, really?'

'Yes. He didn't want me to read it. He took it and ran off, without saying a word.'

'Not even later on?'

'No.'

'And it was after that he took the pistol?'

'Later on I realized the pistol wasn't there any more.' The clarification that follows is minimal, but important, 'That was yesterday afternoon. But I don't know when he took it from the drawer... but yes, it could have been yesterday.'

'After reading that article. So the two things could be related. The article, the pistol...' and then, lowering his voice, '... and the suicide.'

He lifts his head, looks into her eyes.

'Could he have been haunted by some remorse, some guilt? Something stronger than him, from a long time ago?' he suggests quietly, almost as though to himself.

'No. He was a happy man.'

'We can't know that,' says Cataldo, delicately. 'We cannot judge the happiness or the unhappiness of other people.' And death is the ultimate solitary experience, he continues in his own thoughts. Because we are always alone in death.

She coughs now, and she lifts the handkerchief to her mouth. 'Perhaps that's true,' she says, when she can speak.

Of course it is true. He has seen it so often in his work, in his own life. It is true even for those we think we know as well as we know ourselves. No one can ever know what really happens in the final instant of a life. That is why it is not right to judge, but it is right to think. God's heart is bigger than man's heart. And not even a bullet in the head sets us free from ourselves and from the horror. From the infinite hypocrisies and deceits of the world.

CHAPTER FIVE

Eighteen years ago

It is getting even warmer as he leaves the house. Up in the cloudless sky a light aircraft is buzzing around, like a happy fly. But Cataldo is dissatisfied, as he always is when he is just getting started on something new. On the steps he looks up, but there is too much glare, he cannot see any sign of the plane. Then he looks down again and sees the two men from the mortuary in the garden. They are putting the dead man in the green bag; they close the zip and put it in the van. And as they drive out through the gate, he thinks about the fact that he has seen dead men before, but still now, just like the first time, he feels his heart shrink.

There is a fat man standing in the road doing nothing apart from looking at Cataldo. Hands behind his back, belly out, lifting his weight up on tiptoes, then letting it all fall back onto his heels before beginning again. Where has he seen this one before?

'Inspector?'

He had waited until Cataldo came closer to call out to him. What a strange voice – gargling undertones of catarrh.

'Yes?'

'Excuse me, Inspector. I'd like to tell you something...'

Muliere has come upstairs with him and stays for a moment. They introduce themselves, shake hands. Then Cataldo tells Muliere to go back down and wait for him in the car, in front of the hotel, tells him it will not take long and his deputy nods in agreement as he leaves.

They are in the other man's room. He is tall, thin, about forty. And he maybe could be called handsome, with his green eyes, but Cataldo is not interested in that.

'I've heard you were asking about Dr Zoboli the day before yesterday.'

He smiles and says, 'That's right.'

'You said you were his colleague. Is that right too?'

'I did, but it's not true.' He's no longer smiling. 'And I imagine I owe you an explanation.'

'That's a good idea. Since he's dead.'

'Yes, I heard.'

'Already?'

'They're already talking about it,' and with his thumb he points to the floor beneath his feet. 'Some of the guests and the owner. The same guy who told you about me, of course.'

'Of course. And did you find him?'

'Zoboli? No. I asked about him, I got his address, but then I never went there, to his house, and I didn't get to see him.'

'Not even last night?'

He shakes his head, then coughs. 'I was here alone after supper, all night in fact.' And since Cataldo says nothing: 'So I don't have an alibi. Does that matter?'

'Well... that depends.'

'On what?'

'On what else you have to tell me.' And he's uncertain whether to smile or not, but he does as he says, 'You really didn't meet him?'

'No. But I phoned him in the middle of the night and I sent him a photocopy.' And now he smiles. 'I might as well tell you that.'

'Why?'

'It's a long story.'

'I've got all the time you need.'

'Alright then. To start with, my surname isn't Ferrero, it's Marchisio. Alberto really is my first name though, and I really do come from Turin.' He clears his voice, as though getting ready to say something difficult, or preparing to make a jump in time: 'In Turin, eighteen years ago, on 21 February 1980, there was a big fuss when the Carabinieri arrested two Brigate Rosse terrorist leaders – Peci and Micaletto. Do you remember that?'

'No, but go on.'

'On the evening of the twenty-first I was near here, in Vignola... for work. Remember, I was twenty-two years old, I was studying political science and for more than a year I'd been working as an editorial assistant on *Lotta Continua*, the radical magazine in Turin. I was in Vignola when I saw the news on the television. So I phoned a friend of mine who said there was a rumour going round Turin that the police had found papers with names and addresses. At that point I panicked.'

'Why?'

'Firstly because I had met Peci some years previously when I was still at school. It was nothing important – I'd stored some leaflets for him and I'd even put him up for the night once or twice. So I was worried that maybe he might still have my name written somewhere in a notebook, in a diary... among other names, other people very different from me. And then, I did have something on my conscience too.'

'Yes?'

'An old charge, for resisting arrest. During a sit-in, or a march... I really don't remember now. Nothing serious, really, but at the time I didn't see it that way. To cut a long story short, I was so scared I decided to leave that night, hitch-hiking, immediately, I didn't even think of taking the train...'

He tells this story with a thoughtful voice, without feeling, as though digging carefully through his words. And Cataldo leans back in the armchair, hands clasped, silent.

'A guy in a dark blue Mercedes 280S picked me up. I remember him as if it were yesterday. He was about fifty, going back home, to Guiglia... distinguished, well dressed, yes... and he spoke very little, but was very kind...' he coughs before continuing, 'Perhaps he just wanted company. He certainly wasn't afraid of strangers...' and then he adds, quietly, 'Unfortunately.'

'Why unfortunately?'

'Because I was thinking about where I was going – a guest house, a hostel, under an assumed name for two or three days – when at midnight, on the main road to Guiglia, on the Torre bend, we almost crashed into a car that dazzled us as it came in the other direction. It was going fast, too fast, and it was raining a little as well...'

He stops, coughs once or twice and Cataldo continues to wait in silence, concentrated.

'Our car skidded, came off the road and the man who'd given me the lift ended up hitting his head on the windscreen...'

'And you?'

'Completely unharmed. I realized that straight away.'

'You were lucky.'

He doesn't reply, because there's no irony in Cataldo's voice. 'So I looked at him for a moment, I saw that he was bleeding, but he was still breathing. So I got out of the car, instinctively, to look for help...'

'But you didn't call for help.'

'No.' He lowers his eyes, and his voice, 'Because I was frightened...'

'And then?'

'And then I ran off, across the fields, but I turned round and I saw the lights of the other car turning back and I thought, That's good, they'll help him...'

He stops to get his breath and Cataldo notices his shirt is soaked, under his armpits.

'I wandered around all night, not knowing where to go. In the dark, in the rain. They caught me almost immediately, in the morning... I hadn't gone that far, not knowing the area...'

Cataldo closes his eyes and imagines the scene: the wet hair, the stink of sweat, the sweat of fear. And a stranger. Of course they wouldn't have believed him, even if he had had a clean record. When he opens his eyes, he nods.

'You see, don't you? I didn't deny having been in the Mercedes... and the dead man had a wound on his forehead that matched the description of the accident, even though he died from loss of blood and hypothermia. They could certainly have charged me with abandoning him... just as they could have charged them, in the other car.'

'If they'd found them...'

'How do you know they didn't?'

'I didn't. I just imagined what might have happened.'

'You imagined, yes, okay.' He looks down at the floor, at a point between the window and Cataldo's armchair, then he lifts his head and his voice as he looks straight into the Inspector's eyes: 'Do you understand? He died like a dog, alone, and maybe he could have made it... we'll never know... if only they'd done something, phoned a hospital.

But they did nothing.'

'They disappeared.'

'But there's something else. Something more serious.'

Cataldo manages to conceal the first little flash of insight he has had since the story began.

'There was seven hundred million lire in the Mercedes, in a suitcase. The money was never found. And this changed everything.'

'Of course,' Cataldo guesses. 'From failure to assist to murder and robbery.'

'They took my record into account, together with the fact that I'd run off. They said I must have hidden the money somewhere during the night, or that I had an accomplice and that it wasn't true I didn't know the area, since I'd been in Vignola for a few days. It was a quick trial, just a few months, a straightforward one with no doubts, no questions. They sent me down for twenty years, reduced to eighteen for good behaviour. I got out last week.'

There's just one question left now and Cataldo asks it immediately:

'Why did you come back?' And since Marchisio says nothing: 'For the money?'

'No. I'm innocent.'

'For revenge then?'

'No, for justice.'

Cataldo sighs, 'And what is your idea of justice?'

'Justice is a power that never pays for the mistakes it makes. But I meant another type of justice.'

'But it will never repay you for all those lost years.'

'Then let's say that I've come back out of pain.'

'What do you mean?'

'I learned inside that pain doesn't grow old. It floats in your soul, it never sinks.' And after a moment's pause, 'But it's being resigned to pain, to injustice, that kills us for ever.'

Cataldo sighs again as he decides to change the subject.

'Let's get back to the money, if you don't mind. The man, the dead man... what was his name?'

'Cristoni. Walter Cristoni.'

'Okay. What was he doing with all that money?'

'At the trial his wife gave evidence. She knew exactly how much he had with him and she provided proof of the withdrawal from the bank. He was buying an old villa, which was actually worth three times as much, from an estate agency run by a cousin of hers, Tecnodomus it's called.'

'It still exists. Did you see the suitcase?'

'There was a suitcase. He moved it from the passenger seat to the back when I got in. But I don't know what was in it.' And after a pause he adds, 'Really.'

'One more thing. That night... could you have been dazzled deliberately?'

'I've thought about that. It's certainly possible. But to be honest I don't think it was deliberate. Why do you ask?'

'Just an idea.'

It's hot in the room. Cataldo gets up, opens a window and looks outside. Now, under the porticoes, through the glare from the sun and the groups of people, there comes to the hotel the aroma of coffee and voices from the television. And there's a strange atmosphere to it all – tourism and old-town life, a bit sweet, a bit sad.

'Why did you speak about "them" before, when you mentioned the other car?'

He is back in the armchair, having left the window open. Marchisio smiles slightly, 'So you noticed.'

'Yes. You said "they" and then "them". Why?'

'Because there were two of them. And I saw one face. Just a split second, of course, but I saw it well.'

'Even though it was raining?'

'Yes.'

'Are you sure?'

'Yes... I'm telling you, I'm sure!'

'Alright. Calm down. Which one? The driver?'

'No, the other one. The passenger.'

'And...'

'So in prison I took out a subscription to the *Resto del Carlino*, the edition with news from Modena. The hope was that sooner or later I would find that face, the one that's printed here in my mind...' and he touches his forehead with his index finger, 'all through those long days with plenty of time for thinking.'

'I see. And so you found it?'

He nods, then smiles. 'Two years later, when I'd given up all hope.'

Marchisio gets up, goes to the wardrobe, takes out a bag and puts it on the bed. From the bag he pulls out a bulging green folder and when he opens it Cataldo sees it's full of newspaper clippings. He takes one and hands it over: a small article from 1982, from the provincial news section – a party celebrating a graduation, a first class degree with distinction at the age of twenty-four. While Cataldo looks at it, Marchisio moves to his side and points to a face.

'Him?'

Giulio Zoboli, newly graduated, looks out from the photograph – his shirt sleeves rolled, a cigarette held between his fingers. It doesn't take much to understand what happened.

'So you thought that by frightening him with the article about the accident and then tormenting him, he'd take you to the other guy from that night...'

'Yes. We're like snails, didn't you know? We leave trails behind us. And even my car must have frightened him, must have struck some chord. It's the same type, the same model as the one from that night. I searched for it deliberately, to make him react. People had to notice it in town, it had to set alarm bells ringing, so that they'd get in touch. That was what I wanted. Because they must have taken the money, if there was money.'

'And have you found the other man?'

'No, not yet. Because Zoboli died before I could. He shot himself, that's what they were saying downstairs.' He nods, in silence, his gaze lost in his memories. And after a while, almost as though changing subject: 'I read a book in prison. By a poet from Sarajevo, by the name of Osti... I liked it. One poem in particular.'

'Yes?'

'Well... it says that perhaps one day all those left without a grave will come back... one day...' and he coughs during the pause. 'Well... that's what I've been. A dead man without a grave, for eighteen years. But now I'm back.'

'Quite.'

'And my return is a stone thrown into the pond – who knows how far the ripples will go?'

'I see that you like poets.' Cataldo looks at him, without smiling. 'But there's another one. One who said: "Let the dead past bury its dead..."'

'No. I can't do that. I can't come between myself and my past. I can't do that anymore. Because the ghosts have come alive now.'

'Which means?'

'It means that I'm out of prison. And now someone else is

in prison. In the prison called fear.'

The inspector says nothing, so Marchisio adds:

'Fear and remorse. These are the things that give people insomnia. But remorse on its own isn't enough to settle things.'

A fine plan, Cataldo thinks, but full of risks. Even for an intelligent man like this, and with all his patience. Because the truth is like fire, as someone once aptly said: it illuminates, but it also burns. Who knows if Marchisio would understand...

'Do you believe me?'

Cataldo hears the question, and does not reply, but inside he thinks he does believe him. If he is a murderer, or even if he is just a thief, why come back to show his face? Why not simply recover the hidden money and flee? And there was another thing, something even a blind man would have seen.

'Can you lend me your file?' pointing to the folder on the bed. 'For two or three days... no more than that.'

'Of course, go ahead... I know it all by heart.'

And he shakes his hand, sweaty but energetic, and Cataldo is already thinking about the phone call.

He makes it a minute later, in front of the hotel, from the car with Muliere by his side. Just to confirm.

'Was your husband left-handed?'

The answer is almost a whisper, Miriam's yes. There really was no need to ask. After all, Cataldo had just seen the photograph of Zoboli, with that cigarette burning between his fingers.

CHAPTER SIX

School mates

Cataldo has given Muliere a summary of the conversation he just had with Marchisio, up in the hotel room, and he asks:

'What do you think?'

'Of him?'

'Of him and what he's just told me.'

Muliere clears his voice, almost as though he were about to give a speech rather than have a quiet chat with his superior in the car in the shade, Cataldo still with his mobile in his hand. 'To tell you the truth, that Marchisio... I don't know why, but as soon as I saw him there was something I didn't like. Don't you ever just like or dislike someone? On first sight I mean...'

'No. I'm just curious about new people.'

'And as for all the rest, if Zoboli was left-handed and the bullet hole is in the right temple... well, this might actually incriminate Marchisio, rather than clear him...'

'Go ahead.'

'He comes back to get revenge, but he doesn't know that Zoboli's left-handed... which is only logical since they didn't actually know each other. So he kills him in cold blood and tries to make it look like a suicide. Or not?'

'No.' Cataldo shakes his head, without smiling. 'Apart from the fact that Marchisio had a photograph of Zoboli – I've got it here with me – which makes it clear he's left-handed. Just imagine how many times he must have looked at it while he was inside. And revenge is something that's carried out in silence, out of the blue... you don't announce it with phone calls or messages in the mail box. An assassin doesn't usually give two days' notice of his intentions.'

'That's not necessarily true,' Muliere objects. 'For someone who's full of hate, the satisfaction of killing is just too quick. It's better seeing the victim suffer, destroying him slowly with fear...'

'That's right... slowly. Sometimes it works like that, but done slowly it would be over much more than two days and it doesn't add up this way either.' He puts his hands in his pockets, looking for something he cannot find, perhaps his cigarettes. 'And then there are two other things.'

'Which are?'

'The first is that it's unlikely an outsider like Marchisio would have been able to get in to see Zoboli so easily – already worried and suspicious, and that evening he was on his own – and then shoot him in his own home and with his own pistol.'

'And the second thing?'

'By killing Zoboli he'd have lost forever any chance of finding the second guilty man.'

'Unless he'd already found him.'

'Without telling me? Yes, it's possible.' He thinks and looks Muliere in the eye, 'But you know what that means?'

'Sure. Soon we'll have another dead man on our hands.'

'Either Marchisio or the other guy. Exactly. We just have to see who's fastest.'

He gestures with his hand, as though chasing away a nasty thought, but in fact he is just saying goodbye. Behind him, from the open door of the car, comes Muliere's voice:

'Shall I have him kept under surveillance?'

'Yes, that would be best... for the moment at least. I'm

going back in to get something to eat and to have a word with the owner. I'll be in touch with you later.'

There is a quiet room just off a courtyard and it's quite cool in there. Cataldo is sitting at a table with Marchisio's folder in front of him and he is leafing through the cuttings... some of them are very yellowed and fragile, like dried leaves. He has eaten a sandwich and has been here for more than an hour when there is a knock at the door – the hotelier has brought him a beer and hangs around hoping to get a look at the papers. Cataldo closes the folder, puts it away, and then smiles at the other man:

'When someone tells you a true story years after the event, the accuracy of the story is always subjective,' he says, as an opening. 'But there's always a foundation of truth. I mean, it's important to know some facts... to know them in the way they've remained stuck in people's memory... even if those people don't actually remember exactly how things went. Do you follow?'

'I think so,' says the other man, cigarette in hand.

'And it's true that from old stories we might get to hear other things that we hadn't even suspected. Because people speak quite freely about the past, much more than about the present or what happened the day before yesterday. Anyway, that's just something I've noticed over the years.'

'Maybe it's because our memories make us feel younger?'

He smiles, encouragingly. 'Might be. Regarding memories... do you have a good memory?'

'Well... it depends.'

'Let's see then.' Cataldo looks for the right words, and in the meantime runs his thumbnail down the side of the bottle, splitting the wet label in two. 'You've lived here for a long time, haven't you? Do you remember a man called Walter Cristoni, who lived here in Guiglia? A rich guy...'

'Of course I remember. I even met him. But he died... about twenty years ago.'

'Eighteen.'

'If you say so. Anyway, he died... and it wasn't clear what the circumstances were. Is this what you're interested in?'

'Maybe. I still don't know.'

'What do you want to know then?'

'Whether his widow's still in town. She must be about seventy now... she's not necessarily dead...' With his thumb he now draws a circle in the condensation on the bottle, then he pushes it to one side and leans forward, raising his voice slightly, 'I want to know if she still lives in Guiglia, if she remembers anything... if it's worth speaking to her.'

The fat man gestures affirmatively before replying:

'As far as I know, she does still live here... in Via Paganini, near the swimming pool, where they built those new villas. She's very rich. Her husband was in manufacturing, but I can't remember in which particular field. She worked as well... taught history, I remember that because she used to write articles for *Guiglia Oggi*, the local tourist board's magazine. By the way, if you're interested I'll introduce you to the secretary of the tourist board – Nunzio's his name, comes here sometimes to play billiards. But it might be quicker if you go to the office, it's just round the corner, in Via Roma. There's no phone, but in the summer it's always open... for the holidaymakers, in the evening too.'

'Is it open tonight?'

'I think so.'

'And do you think it's worth going to see the widow Cristoni?'

'I'd say so. She's always been an intelligent, well read woman.'

Cataldo gets up from the table to get out of the sun. The other man continues: 'She had one son – Marco, who went off to university. But he never graduated, lived off his family's money, went off the rails...'

'Gambling or women?' Cataldo guesses.

'Heroin. That's how he died. He'd be about forty now...'

'More or less my age.'

'Sorry?'

'No, nothing. It's strange though.'

'What's strange?'

'That he wasn't at his father's funeral. I looked carefully at the photos,' and with his index finger he points to the closed folder, 'and he's not in any of them. It wasn't until a week after the funeral that he reappeared, helped with enquiries... very strange.'

Cataldo drinks a sip of the beer, savouring it slowly – the bottle is half full and the beer is warming up.

'Have I been of any help?' the fat man asks suddenly.

'We'll see.' He looks at him and smiles again. 'But you've given me an idea... and I need ideas. Sometimes they turn out to be wrong, other times they're right... but at least they get us moving.'

'As long as you're happy... can I get you anything else?'

'No, thanks. You can go. If I need you I'll get in touch.'

He has left his cigarette in the ashtray and a thin line of bluish smoke rises, the ash still hanging. Cataldo opens the folder again and starts reading, looking at his watch now and then.

So here we go again, he thinks. The usual ritual of the interview – the litany of questions, the scrutiny of people's characters, the subtle game of pauses, gazes – all this taking place in the theatre that is the interview room. The search for a sign, some uneasiness or a mistake that might lead to the case being closed. And as always he will notice in others their surprise at the discrepancy between his surname and his appearance – a tall, blonde southerner, not stocky and dark-haired, not even authoritarian and not a dialect speaker. He can of course just ignore all this, or he can make a joke out of it... perhaps mentioning the fact that many Sicilians have Norman ancestors. This is the game that will be played till the very end.

Via Dante Alighieri again – the last house, the gate closed. He buzzes and she comes to the door almost immediately, without even asking who it is on the intercom. Perhaps she saw him from a window, behind the curtains, or perhaps not; perhaps she knew he would be back.

'Please come in.'

Cataldo looks at her back as she leads the way. Just below the nape of her neck, her skin curves into a soft dimple... partly hidden by her straight hair.

'Do you have more questions for me?'

She points to the sofa in the cool of the living room, then she sits opposite, in an armchair. And before he replies they look at each other in silence for a moment and it seems to him that her eyes express no feeling. Two serious eyes with something absent in them, something impersonal. Grief, probably...

'I was struck by your call just before. When you asked me if Giulio was left-handed...'

However lucky you are in your life, you will not be spared the experience of grief... where had he read that phrase once?

'So, do you have something else to ask me?'

He focuses, smiles. 'There is something, yes. I'm sorry, but I'd like to know if you have any memory of one night in February, eighteen years ago.'

Suddenly she becomes serious. 'Why so far back?'

'Because the photocopy from the *Carlino*, the one you told me about, refers to this particular night. There was an accident at midnight, just outside Guiglia – everyone knew about it.'

'Ah...'

'A businessman died, a man called Cristoni, and a suitcase containing seven hundred million lire went missing from his car. A hitchhiker was convicted, sent down for a long time, but he's always maintained his innocence...' He looks her in the eye. 'Didn't you know about this?'

'No, I told you. I didn't even read that photocopy... I only caught a glimpse of it.'

In the half-light of the room, with the shutters closed, it seems to him that she blushes, and that he can hear a different note in her voice.

'That's true. You did tell me. But you must recall it now.'

She breathes deeply, then nods. 'Yes, I remember it. Everything. But how did you...'

'How did I come to know about it? Marchisio told me... the hitchhiker. He's the one who put the photocopy in the mail box. He's done eighteen years for that death, then been released, and now he's here.'

Perhaps she understands, or perhaps she wants to ask why, but she doesn't. She just lowers her eyes and when she speaks again her voice is definitely different, almost hoarse.

'You're right. Everyone in town was talking about it. We

did too.'

'We?'

'The seven of us. Our group. That very evening we'd celebrated Ramondini's graduation, he's one of us, at the Tre
Lune, a restaurant that's still there... on the main road to
Vignola, six or seven kilometres from where the accident
took place. It was a nice party, very cheerful, but then the
next day...'

'You read about it in the newspapers, I understand. Tell me
about Ramondini.'

'Luigi. He's forty-three, a bachelor. He's the one who's had
the most successful career – he's already a full Professor at
the university...'

'I see, a brainbox. And apart from you, who else was there?
Your husband?'

'Giulio was there, yes.' For just an instant a shadow runs
through her voice. 'We were going out at the time. He was
twenty-two, studying literature in Bologna. Giulio is... was...
three years younger than Ramondini, but you wouldn't have
noticed. They were great friends even at high school. We all
went to the same school...' she speaks quietly, sometimes
almost as though she is talking to herself, '... the Muratori,
in Modena, section B. I know Giulio had helped Luigi with
his dissertation, with his research...'

'Pardon my curiosity, but if you were all from Modena,
why did you choose to celebrate here in Guiglia? Had it
been summer, I might have understood...'

'Because we'd all been coming here on holiday since we
were children. We liked it here. My parents even had their
wedding reception here. For us it was a nice place. And then
I...' and she blushes now, undecided, 'I even did some painting. Years ago. When I first saw these hills I thought they

were boring, then I understood that all it took was a ray of light, a gust of wind, and they opened up, they moved...'

Cataldo nods. 'I'd like to see one. Really. And did the others like your paintings?'

'The others?' She is surprised. 'I don't know. They never said anything.' And after a moment: 'The others... yes. I still have to tell you about them... there was Don Lodi, Athos Lodi that is. Do you know him?'

'No. Should I?'

'Well, he has a publishing house in Modena and a cultural foundation that's named after him here in Guiglia. He's from Guiglia, but we met him in Modena.'

'At school?'

'That's right. He was our history and philosophy teacher, then he became something of a... of a cultural mentor for us. At university, and even after we'd graduated...'

'I'll have to meet him then. From the way you speak about him.'

'Yes, you should. He's in his fifties – very well read and very generous. Especially with young people. And he was fond of Giulio...'

Her voice cracks, and Cataldo hurries on.

'Who else was there?'

'Ah... yes, Carlo Zanetti. He was at school with us too, as was Katia, his wife – they first met in class. But he never went to university, he was keen on football. He played, you know...'

'And was Katia there?'

'Yes, she was there too. They were going out together, like me and Giulio. None of us were married.'

'I understand. What's she like?'

'Katia? She's intelligent. Better read than her husband. She wanted to study, even went to university, but she gave up, never got her degree...'

'Why?'

'Because he didn't care for studying and it rubbed off on her... that's how I see it. The fact is, she gave up and she regretted it.' She stops, looks at him and then adds, 'They have one son, he's at primary school now.'

'There's still one more.'

'Yes, Calabrese was there too. I don't think you know him...'

'No.'

'Francesco Calabrese. Bachelor. Degree in economics, an accountant, rich and intelligent. Nice house, here in Guiglia, Lancia K 2000, customized. How's that for a description?'

'Lucky him. Strange though...'

'What?'

'That I haven't noticed a car like that in town.'

'Because he doesn't drive very much. It's understandable. He's disabled.' She lowers her voice, as if out of respect, as if Calabrese were there listening. 'At home he uses a wheel-chair.'

'Ah... and why?'

'Polio, as a child. There was no treatment then, not even the vaccine. But I don't know any more than that. And then he transferred to our school in the third year.'

'So you don't know him as well. I mean, as well as you know the others. Good.' Cataldo sighs, stretches his legs, then crosses them. 'Yes, I'd like you to give me their addresses before I go. Do you think I'll be able to get hold of all of them?'

'Right now, yes. They either live here, or they're here for the holidays.'

There is a pause. And she looks around, as though uneasy about something.

'I'm sorry, I haven't offered you anything... a coffee?'

He smiles as he looks at her.

'I've got an espresso machine... or perhaps you'd like a cold drink?'

'Thank you, but I've almost finished.' He shakes his head, politely, then leans back in the armchair. 'So what do you remember, then, of that evening?'

'Very little, unfortunately. It was a long time ago...'

'I know, but even that very little might be useful.'

'Really?'

'You never know.'

She concentrates in silence and he does nothing to disturb her, showing not a single sign of impatience. Only for a moment does he find himself distracted by the sight of her legs, then he averts his eyes and waits, also because the momentary distraction has suddenly brought back a memory.

Miriam, too, has remembered something: 'It started at eight o'clock, or thereabouts. A party for a group of friends in a private room... something to eat, the cake and some spumante. It was all very merry... maybe a little too merry.'

Cataldo has an idea. 'Do you have any photographs?'

'I'm not sure, but I think so... yes, Ramondini must have them. He was keen on keeping photographs as souvenirs...'

'That makes sense. After all, it was his celebration.'

'And a photographer came. Yes, now I remember... a photographer from the tourist office, for their magazine, which is called...'

'*Guiglia Oggi.*'

'Do you know it?'

'No, but someone just mentioned it.'

'Oh yes? It's just a small, local thing... but Ramondini has always been a bit on the vain side, it could even have been him who asked them to write a piece...'

'With a photograph.' Cataldo smiles at this display of human weakness. 'But why did you say before that there was too much merriment?'

'Because of Giulio.' She is more serious now, and she looks towards a point on the floor, somewhere to rest her eyes. 'He was euphoric, excited... I don't know. It was as if Ramondini's graduation had infected him with some sort of frenzy. As if he was the one graduating. Or maybe he was just thinking about his own future graduation... the fact is that he started drinking.'

'Even though the priest was there?'

'Yes. It's strange, isn't it? But that's what happened. He'd never done that before...'

'And did he leave alone?'

'Not at all. He left with me... at about eleven. I drove. He was too tipsy to drive.'

Cataldo looks at her firmly.

'I have to tell you something. Marchisio says he saw him. He wasn't driving, it's true... he was in a car with someone. But it was midnight, not eleven.' And since Miriam says nothing, 'Do you understand? One hour later.'

'That's impossible!' She suddenly raises her voice, her face red, almost ugly. 'And then, if he'd seen Giulio in the car with me...'

'He didn't say he'd seen him with you... he didn't see who was driving. He only saw your husband.'

'And why didn't he tell the police? Why not at the trial?'

'Because he only discovered who it was later, after the

trial, when he was in prison.'

'And you believe him?'

'It's still too early to say... I'm only at the beginning of this. But you, are you sure of the time?'

'Yes, I told you. Positive.'

'Alright.'

As he gets up and shakes her hand, he has not decided whether to believe her or not. Her face now is a bit too rigid, her eyes slightly veiled. Lies, of course, can change people's features in this way, but so can tension in an innocent person.

'Will you come back again?' She asks suddenly, when they are at the door.

'To ask you more questions?'

'Yes.'

He looks at her. 'That depends.'

'On what?'

'On you.'

It seems to Cataldo that she smiles, but people always smile when they fail to understand something.

CHAPTER SEVEN

The priest

'I remember that evening. It seems odd, but I do, even though it was so long ago. The fact is we were celebrating the graduation of Luigi, one of my best pupils. Perhaps that's why it has stayed in my mind...'

Don Lodi is certain as they sit in the library of the Foundation, and Cataldo immediately thinks he has done the right thing in coming here to see him, so serious and authoritative does he appear. Especially at the beginning of an investigation there is a real need for reliable witnesses. Three walls of the room are taken up with matching bookshelves: the books with their ivory colour, the shelves in warm oak and the room itself is austere – all these tangible signs of culture lend this meeting, these words, a comforting atmosphere of truth, or at least of reliability.

'And I imagine you must have had many pupils. I mean you know all about young people...'

'Yes, I'd say so.' He smiles, pleased, and then proceeds to speak as though reciting some maxim, 'When a youngster's setting out, he's betting on himself, on his future. On what he'll manage to do as a grown man.'

'And Ramondini?'

'Ramondini graduated at twenty-five, which would not have been anything special, but he wrote a fine dissertation on Nievo... on some minor works by Nievo. The *Novelliere Campagnuolo*, and part of his thesis was published immediately in *Belfagor*, the journal.' His eyes sparkle behind his glasses, 'A wonderful debut, no doubt about it.'

72

'And you had foreseen this?'

'Yes, I was right about him, about all of them, from the very beginning.'

'From their school days?'

'That's right. I don't say that out of pompousness, believe me, but simply because I understand young people, just as you said. Ramondini has a successful career, but Giulio too... I mean Zoboli, was just as good. In fact, in many ways he was sharper, more... intuitive, let's say.'

'But.'

'But he was less sure of himself. Less confident, and a bit more fragile too. Ramondini has always been more of a hard worker, more reliable, totally concentrated on his work... partly because he's on his own. No women, for example, to distract him.'

'Are you referring to Zoboli's wife?'

'I'm referring to the fact that study, research, has to be a vocation. Something exclusive, which cannot be compromised by anything else.'

He makes a gesture, as though wanting to take his glasses off, then he simply settles them on his nose, while Cataldo wonders, for the first time, if the priest's judgement of his pupils is perhaps related in equal parts to his high level of industry and to a high degree of misogyny.

'That's the way it was from school onwards,' he repeats, 'then university confirmed it. Their destiny was already there in their characters.'

'Do you really believe that?'

'Yes, because I've always been close to them. Culturally, in their work... right up to today. Partly because the town is a small one, partly because of the Foundation I run. And the publishing house.'

'I've been told about that.'

'Oh yes?' he smiles, proudly. 'I created both of them. And I've never stopped taking care of them. Not even now.'

'As though they were children,' says Cataldo and he almost regrets saying it, but he doesn't know why.

'Do you have children, Inspector?'

'Me? No.'

'I understand.' He walks round the table and when he starts speaking again, he seems to have changed the subject, but Cataldo knows he hasn't and knows that this time he had better not interrupt him. 'I always tell my students, my youngsters, that they have to learn to control the whims, to dominate inconstancy, to be patient too, in order to acquire an understanding of the sense of one's life. To be able finally to love something.' He looks around, makes a slight gesture in the air. 'Here... I have loved all this.'

There is some exaggeration, perhaps, in his tone. But Cataldo nods.

'The books, the research. A publishing house, which belongs to me.'

'Why?'

'Why? Because a man is his desires. Because it is through our desires that we experience life. Because writing, publishing, is like deceiving death, letting the best part of us live on.' He coughs now – once, twice – and he turns red in the face. 'And a publisher is a man who offers another man a map that will never die, a map for exploring his present and his past.'

There follows a silent pause. And when he hears his own voice, Cataldo feels that the atmosphere of this discourse has infected him too, infected his words:

'But we are books. People who fall ill, wither and are forgotten... yes, this too. They are images of our lives...'

'No, that's not it!' the priest raises his voice, his eyes motionless, his knuckles white for a moment as he tightens his fists. 'That's not true. Because what you write, what you publish, remains. And it's possible to garner something, of men, of life... above and beyond time, beyond memory.'

He swallows, he lowers his eyes. It would be highly instructive, thinks Cataldo, to listen to some more. But it's time to return to more concrete ground.

'And did they see it that way too?'

'Who?'

'Zoboli and Ramondini, for example.'

'Yes, yes they did.'

'And the others?'

'Oh... the others...' and he smiles slightly now, in a superior manner. 'All good folk, excellent, as people... but with different talents.'

'Carlo Zanetti?'

'Him... at school he was a real dunce, but he was good at football. He even had something of a career in it, but I don't know much about that. Now he runs an estate agency, here in town... Tecnodomus.'

'I've heard it mentioned. Did it exist eighteen years ago?'

'Yes, it was owned by a chap from Guiglia, a cousin of Signora Cristoni. Cristoni, the businessman's widow... the man who had that accident. Two of them bought Tecnodomus, I don't know when – Zanetti and Calabrese.'

'Oh yes?'

He nods. 'They sat together in class at high school. Have you met Calabrese?'

'Not yet.'

'He was good at school, especially at maths, despite the fact ours was a classics school. In fact he went on to get a degree in economics and now he's an accountant.'

'An intelligent man...'

'Yes, and he knows it.' He looks at a point in the air, as if to reflect better. 'He loves to feel himself to be intelligent, but this doesn't help him feel any happier.'

'Why?'

'Because of his disability. Polio, as a child...'

'Ah, yes. I've been told.'

'A disability, I was saying, which he tries to compensate for with his pride, with professional success, but it's obvious to everyone and he can't forget it...' He stops there and then adds, 'That's one of the reasons why he's so close to Zanetti.'

'What do you mean?'

'Because Zanetti has what Calabrese lacks. A physique, sport... and women. He admired him... he still admires him.'

'And Zanetti needs his brains. I see. And that's how they became partners...'

'Yes. Equals.'

'Fifty-fifty,' says Cataldo. 'What type of company is Tecnodomus?'

'A private company, I think... with one office here and one in Vignola. They operate mostly in our Apennine area.'

'Is it doing well?'

'I don't know any of the details, but I think so, yes. Why?'

'Nothing. I was just thinking that buying it must have cost a tidy sum...'

'That's possible. But Calabrese has always had plenty of money.' He looks at Cataldo. 'Did you know that too?'

'I had heard something along those lines, yes. From Miriam...'

'Ah, her. I have no doubt she's well informed. She always

knows everything, that one...'

Something in Lodi's tone strikes him. It is a shame he cannot probe deeper.

'So he's really rich, then?'

'An inheritance, I think. Then he made investments – the stock exchange, or at least that's what they say. I know nothing about Zanetti's money.'

'When did they buy it?'

'The agency? I've already told you I don't know.'

'After the accident?'

'Cristoni's accident? Yes, certainly. A few years after.' From behind the glasses now comes a teasing look, 'You could always ask Miriam...'

'I'll ask Calabrese.' He is not going to probe into the priest's attitude towards Miriam, it's not the right moment. 'I thought I'd pay a visit, to the agency.'

'But he never goes there, he just put the money into it.'

And the brains, obviously. Cataldo thanks him: 'You did the right thing in telling me, I'll go to his house. And Zanetti?'

'Yes, he's always there.'

'With his wife?'

'No, why?'

'I just thought she probably helped him...'

'No, no. She stays at home, with their son.'

'She doesn't work?'

'No. She went to university, she was good. But then she dropped out.'

He doesn't ask why because he knows Lodi will tell him anyway.

'Not such a great couple, that one. In fact they've both hurt each other, and they know it. He basically made her give up her studies because he wasn't interested, and she made him marry her, falling pregnant when he seemed to be a good catch with the mirage of the football career. Even though she lost the child...'

Cataldo cannot decide if he is unbelievably frank or unbelievably misogynistic, but he decides anyway to play the game.

'I think I understand the type. A bright girl, basically honest, but ready to make the most of any opportunities that come her way. Is that right?'

'More or less, yes.'

'What's more she's pretty, and the pretty girls usually have more opportunities than the others...'

'I don't know about Katia, but I think you're right. I say that on the basis of logic, you understand... certainly not on the basis of my experience, which is most limited.'

Cataldo smiles in order to defuse (or at least to try to) a certain tension he perceives now, as they gradually get closer to the final words, the crucial ones, the ones with which someone contradicts himself, or makes a mistake. Or lies.

'To change the subject. You know that Marchisio, the stranger in town, told me he saw Zoboli in a car at midnight at the Torre bend... at the scene of the accident, while Miriam swears she went home from the party with him an hour before?'

'I don't remember when and with whom he went home.' He stares at something far off, in the void, or beyond the open window, trying to remember, to concentrate, but it is just an instant. 'I really don't know. In fact, I can't know because I left the party first. She said at eleven?'

'Yes, at eleven o'clock.'

'Ah, yes. I'd already left, I'm sure of it.'

'Why?'

'Because it was a Saturday and on the Sunday morning I had to be at Stresa for a conference on Rebora.' He stops and smiles proudly. 'I had a paper to present, you see? My first paper at a conference, that's why I still remember.'

'Rebora?' says Cataldo quietly, slightly puzzled.

'Yes. "A Reading of the Lyrical Fragments", that was the title. A mixture of theology and literature...'

Cataldo stares at him, carefully, and the other man continues as though flattered.

'I went through his development as a poet, between faith and reason. Or rather between rationalistic illumination and divine communion.' He smiles again. 'So I went to bed early.'

He must have been a good teacher, judging by the language and the passion. And in private a man with a complex, articulated personality. I have never met such a multifaceted person, thinks Cataldo, and at the same time he has a fundamental coherence to him. But in those last words – or at some other moment in their talk, he cannot remember – he also picked up on a slight cracking of the voice, almost a fear. That was the impression he had.

'I've heard that a photographer came from the tourist office to take some pictures that evening. Do you remember that?'

'Vaguely... yes, someone came.'

'And an article was published...'

He opens his arms, almost pathetically, 'I don't know. I really don't know. And where is it supposed to have appeared?'

'In *Guiglia Oggi*, perhaps. That's what they say.'

'That's why then. Decidedly not something I read. And it

must be a limited circulation publication...'

'I think you're right. I wonder if Nunzio might have it, in the library... but it doesn't matter.'

They shake hands, Cataldo thanks him and says that will be all for now.

He has already decided where he is going. And he is pleased it is nearby, pleased to be able to go there on foot, to stretch his legs and do some thinking. And immediately something strange jumps into his mind as he is walking along Via Di Vittorio, in the afternoon heat. Despite all the initial caution and reluctance, it is strange that two people remember so well, with so many details, a supper from eighteen years ago. Experience has taught him, however, just how much reality is distorted and even wiped out, when filtered through the suggestions of time. And yet, despite the many memories, there is still a good part of that evening and that night missing from the record. But a part of anything can be broken into fragments, and these fragments can be found one by one with the tenacious application of patience. Yes, it is just a matter of patience.

CHAPTER EIGHT

The beautiful woman

It is in Via Del Voltone, behind the pine wood and there is not much to it, seen from the outside. It almost makes you think he cannot be doing very well. A two-storey building, which once upon a time must have been white but now is a dirty grey and near the top of the walls has a wide brown band, a stain from the rusting gutter.

When he rings the doorbell, a woman's voice replies on the intercom: 'Just a minute,' as the door buzzes open. He nods, starts climbing the stairs and hears her voice getting closer as he rises. She is on the phone, and when he reaches the landing he can see her too, her shoulders, through the half-open door. He stops and waits.

She carries on talking – perhaps she cannot cut the conversation short, perhaps she doesn't realize he is already upstairs, standing behind her. He could cough, certainly, call her attention to himself, but he prefers listening in silence, soaking up her gestures, the tone of her voice. Just like that, with no particular motive.

She has a French 'r' and a girl's voice – much younger than her forty years. Squeaky, confident. Then she feels his gaze on her, she turns, gestures hello, lowers her voice. 'I have to go,' she whispers. 'I'll call you back.' It is a shame he cannot ask whom she was speaking to.

Standing on the threshold, she studies Cataldo's badge then gives it back to him, moving to one side to let him in. Then she closes the door.

She looks him in the eye for a moment in the entrance and

she clears her throat, as though she is a bit hoarse, or as though she is about to make a long speech, but she remains silent. Maybe it is just out of shyness, prudence, who knows? She straightens her summer dress – light cloth, with a floral print – it's all creased and clinging to her, as though she has been out in the sticky heat and has just got back. As she does so, however, she catches sight of herself in the mirror on the wall, grimaces as she notes how dishevelled she is. Cataldo says nothing.

'Come in,' she says eventually. And he sits on a two-seater sofa, looking around in the tiny living room of an apartment that seems as small and neglected as he had guessed it would be, from looking at the building from out on the street. Then she sits too, in the armchair facing the sofa, again not saying a word. For a moment, possibly to hide her impatience or her embarrassment, she plays with an earring – just the one, turquoise, that she had taken off who knows when – then she puts it back on her right ear. Cataldo does nothing to break the silence, rather he savours it because it allows him to observe this woman, to place her in her home. No trick, no errors in perspective.

'Can I help you?'

She is a beautiful woman, more so than Miriam. Her honey-blonde hair is the first thing that strikes him – combed straight on either side of a central parting and cut between her ears and her shoulders. And the long eyelash-es, and the deep, dark eyes. Cataldo thinks she still looks like a student, except for those small crows' feet around the eyes.

'Yes.'

'Is it... about Zoboli?'

'Yes, it's about him. I know you were friends.'

'Something like that.'

'So I was hoping, coming here... that you might help me understand what type of person he was – his character, his personality.'

'To understand what type of person he was?' She lowers her eyes, shakes her head. 'I'm sorry, but I can't help you.'

'Why?'

'Because I didn't know him that well. We were only at school together. Then later at university, Faculty of Letters. No, I didn't know him very well... assuming you can ever know anyone well.' And since Cataldo says nothing: 'We were only at university together at the very beginning, because I dropped out...'

'So I've been told.'

'So you understand?'

During the pause that follows she stands up, taking the cushion out from behind her back as she does so and holding it in her hands, as though in need of comfort.

He offers her a cigarette. 'You don't smoke? Good for you. So you were saying that Giulio...'

'Zoboli, yes... I didn't see him often. When I think that he's dead now...'

But even a blind man would see that she has been crying. Her red, spent eyes are a giveaway, as are the swollen face and the red patches round her cheeks. Why?

'As far as you know, did he have any enemies?'

The word takes her by surprise.

'Zoboli? Enemies? What do you mean?'

'Enemies to the point where they'd want to kill him'

'I don't know... but didn't he kill himself?'

'We have to wait for the post-mortem, Signora. We can't just decide that.'

Suddenly she is afraid. She pulls the cushion to her breast, instinctively, almost as though it were a child in need of protection.

'Why? Is it possible he was killed?'

'I didn't say that. Just that we don't have the report yet.'

'Ah...'

'Another thing, while I'm here. Eighteen years ago... the night of 21 February 1980 to be precise, there was a fatal accident near here. A businessman, Cristoni, came off the road on the Torre bend and a suitcase containing seven hundred million lire went missing from the car. Who knows how much it would be worth today.' He looks at her, seriously. 'Did you ever hear about it?'

'Something about it, yes...'

'In fact that night you were all nearby, celebrating Ramondini's graduation. Remember?'

She runs a hand through her hair and seems undecided, almost as though she doesn't really remember that evening, but she understands how difficult it must be to make him believe her.

'It was a long time ago...'

'Please try just the same. He was the first one in your group to graduate...'

With an elbow leaning on the armrest of the sofa, he looks at her and waits. There is not the smallest sign of impatience in the relaxed composure of his features.

'I... I can't remember anything. Nothing at all, I'm sorry...'

'Not even what time you left?'

'Not even that, no.' And now in the pause there is a flash of uncertainty in her eyes.

'It's not important, is it?'

'No,' says Cataldo, quietly. 'I don't think it's important.'

He is not sure, as he stands up, whether he was looking to

reassure her or to keep her from being suspicious. He knows there are other things he should be asking her, but for the moment this is enough. It has been years now since he last rushed his interviews. Ever since he learnt that his profession really does require large doses of patience.

She accompanies him to the door and leans on a radiator there. Next to her, on the wall, hangs a reproduction of a still life: Giorgio De Chirico, *I Frutti di Nettuno*, oil on canvas, late 1920s, recites Cataldo mentally, without pride, because De Chirico is his favourite artist. In silence she follows the line of his gaze. 'My husband likes it very much,' she says, before closing the door. And he thinks for a moment, then decides not to. He is not going to tell her that her husband is his next visit.

The afternoon is almost over and Tecnodomus is probably about to close when Cataldo arrives: there is no one inside, behind the glass doors. A very simple office, he thinks – no more than two or three rooms. The desk is tidy, the computer is switched off, a few brochures on a low table to the right, next to the coffee machine. And there is a moveable noticeboard, a bit like a blackboard, with lots of coloured squares on it, displaying the month's special offers. He takes a look, out of habit: apartments, second homes, but country homes too – Guiglia, Vignola and Marano. Then suddenly he hears voices. Two men are coming out of a room. He knows there is no good reason, but something leads him not to say hello, not to cough even. He stands there listening. They do not sense that they are observed, they continue to speak. Utterly engrossed, in a low voice, even though they are alone – standing in the corridor, just ten metres away and they still have not seen him. One is tall, thin, wearing jacket and tie despite the heat, and a pair of glasses with heavy frames that make him look older than he is. Glasses for long-sightedness, certainly, since he has a sheet of paper or something in his hand and he continues looking at it as he speaks. The other man is about forty, slightly shorter without being small, but he is more athletic, muscular, with his shirt open to his waist, a handsome face and the confident air of a sportsman or a playboy. It's the other one who looks more worried, bent forward, speaking out of the corner of his mouth, with that paper in his hand, the paper that he would like to keep hold of and the other one is waiting to see. No, this guy has not come to discuss a house purchase.

Finally they see him. They move and the shorter one folds the paper and puts it in his pocket as Cataldo advances towards them.

'Signor Zanetti?'

'That's me. How can I help you?'

'Inspector Cataldo.' He shows the badge to both of them after which there is a pause, the exchange of glances, the unease. The usual ritual.

'It'll be about Zoboli,' says Zanetti, as though speaking to himself. 'Of course. He's dead and you're doing the rounds of his friends.' Then he looks directly at Cataldo and his voice is louder as he says, 'Please, come in. Have you been waiting long?'

'No, not at all. I've only just arrived, I was taking a look around.'

He nods towards the noticeboard with the offers: 'Interesting...'

'But you're not here for that. And I don't want to waste your time. By the way...' he turns and gestures with his hand. 'Let me introduce a friend, Professor Ramondini.'

'Pleased to meet you,' says Cataldo, shaking a damp and cold hand: 'Luigi Ramondini?'

'Yes... why?'

'Nothing,' he smiles. 'Just that I've heard your name mentioned.'

'Oh yes?' And he does not ask by whom or where, and he does not seem relieved; he appears rather alert, or tense. And there is a deep line, running from his nostrils to his cheeks, which gives the impression of a sad smile.

'Come on, let's sit down,' says Zanetti, cordially, even a bit too cordially, and, as though to confirm his willingness to speak with Cataldo, he goes to the glass door and locks it. 'In any case, that's it for this afternoon...' he says, smiling, as he returns. Then he takes two metal chairs, moves them in front of the desk and gestures invitingly with his hand. 'Would you like a coffee?' he asks before sitting down.

So they have a coffee from the machine, all of them sitting close to one another, like people who have taken a friend to the train station and are staying until the departure time out of good manners. Some slight embarrassment, perhaps even diffidence. Until Cataldo breaks the silence.

'Can you guess where I've just been, Signor Zanetti?'

'No idea.'

'Your house. I've just spoken with your wife.'

'With Katia? Really? And how did she take that?' he says, smiling. 'Did you scare her?'

'No... why should she be scared?'

'Are you married, Inspector?'

Cataldo smiles now: 'Unfortunately I haven't had your luck.'

'Well... I'm not sure luck comes into it. But if you were

married you'd know that women are a bit strange. My wife once had a fit when the traffic police stopped her, just imagine her reaction to a Detective Inspector... that's what I meant.'

'She seemed a bit worried, yes. But not scared. And maybe worried isn't really the right word.'

'Just as well.'

'For her, but not for me. She wasn't really of much use.'

'Why?'

'Well... she doesn't remember much about your friend's graduation party...' And he gestures towards Ramondini, turning to look at him, to involve him in the conversation. But the professor says nothing, he just leans forward after a few seconds, rubbing his palms on his knees, almost as though his hands are sweating.

'Why that supper?' asks Zanetti, speaking up for his friend. 'It was so long ago...'

But he does not seem surprised, or at least really surprised and Cataldo decides to provide a brief summary, with one or two added details.

'The thing is... be it suicide or not, Zoboli is dead, but the strange thing is that he died straight after the arrival of Signor Marchisio here in Guiglia. Perhaps the name means nothing to you... or perhaps it does. He's the hitchhiker who eighteen years ago was convicted of the murder of a businessman, Cristoni was his name, and of the theft of seven hundred million lire from Cristoni's car. All this took place at the Torre bend, 21 February 1980. At midnight.'

'And so?'

'So that's where you come in. First, because that evening, just a few kilometres away, you were all celebrating the professor's graduation...'

'That's true,' says Ramondini, eventually.

'Ah... so you do remember?'

'Of course I do...'

'And what do you remember precisely?'

'That I left when the waiter was clearing the table. I was the last to go...'

'Yes?'

'Because I had to pay the bill...'

'Of course, it was your treat.' And Cataldo laughs heartily, followed by the other two. 'That's good to know.'

Then he turns serious again and picks up on where he had left off in the story: 'The thing is that Marchisio has said something very interesting... he maintains that Cristoni came off the road because he was dazzled by a car that was travelling towards Vignola. He didn't see who was driving, but he did see Zoboli in the passenger seat. And that's not all...'

'No?' asks Zanetti, but says nothing more. Ramondini, in the meantime, has pulled out a cigarette and has tried twice to light it, but with no joy and in the end he puts cigarette and lighter back in his pocket.

'No. Marchisio says that the car turned back, while he was running away, having left Cristoni dying in his car.'

'And do you believe him?' asks Zanetti spontaneously. 'You believe a man who runs away, leaving another man more dead than alive?'

'Yes... yes, I have to believe him. Otherwise he wouldn't have come back here.'

Suddenly silence falls in the office. When Zanetti eventually speaks, his voice is different, almost hoarse.

'And what has he come back to do?'

'To look for the driver.' The answer this time has come

from Ramondini, quietly, patiently. Now he looks at Cataldo and adds, 'Am I right?'

'I think you know.'

'Why do you say that?'

'Because you're intelligent. And you already understand that the driver stole the money from the car. The driver, together with Zoboli.' Cataldo pauses and stares at both of them. 'And now Zoboli is dead.'

'Just a moment... this guy, this... what's his name?'

'Marchisio.' Cataldo and Ramondini both say.

'Right. Him,' Zanetti almost shouts. 'But what proof does this Marchisio have? After so many years?'

'Forget that.' says Ramondini, tiredness in his voice. 'Rather, what chance is there of identifying the driver... as he says... after so many years?'

'Very little chance, of course. But I'm trying.'

'Are there any witnesses?'

'There is one, yes.'

'Can I... can we...' he looks at Zanetti, who nods nervously, '... know who it is?'

'Of course. It's Zoboli's widow.'

'Miriam?'

'Yes, Miriam. Are you surprised?' They do not reply, so he adds: 'She says she was driving, because he'd drunk a bit, at the supper. Do either of you remember that?'

'I don't,' says Zanetti.

'I don't either,' says the other. 'So then...'

'So then where's the problem, you mean? Well, there is a big problem. Because Miriam admits to having driven, but one hour before the accident took place. She maintains she left the party at eleven, not at twelve o'clock. And that doesn't add up.'

'Ah!' exclaims Zanetti now, and the other two both look at him in surprise. Something has passed across his face, suddenly – amazement or sudden interest, or who knows what. For a moment it is as though he is trying to recall, to drag up some memory. Then his expression relaxes, and he smiles once again.

'Has something come to mind?'

'Yes. Miriam and Giulio really did leave together. But I know nothing more than that... I mean, I don't know if it was eleven... just as I don't know if Giulio was able to drive or not. I didn't realize he was drunk...'

'Just a bit merry, in truth.' Cataldo sighs. 'And you, Professor?'

'Me?'

'Do you remember anything of that evening? You might be able to. After all, it was your party.'

'No, I don't think so.' He concentrates (or is he pretending?). 'Nothing in particular.' And then, after a pause, with a smile, 'Is that serious?'

'That depends on Marchisio.'

He notes Ramondini's questioning, smiling look and then adds, as he stands up: 'Because if he's told the truth and if he continues to do the rounds here in town, someone else could be in danger.'

The smile, be it of embarrassment or momentary light-heartedness, has died on Ramondini's lips and the line between his nose and his jawbone becomes deeper, darker. He is worried, but he deserves to be, and if he knows something he would do himself a favour by spitting it out. And it is just as well he still has time to do so. That's what Cataldo thinks as he takes his leave, the other two men left staring at his back.

In the heat of the late afternoon as he walks towards the car park, Cataldo now has the same thought that often comes to him after an interview or a meeting, one of those that leave him dissatisfied, without really knowing why. It really would be great to be a fly on the wall, or a god – someone who picks up on everything that has to do with other people. Even their dreams and their memories and the loves of their lives... their cowardly actions, their ignoble scheming. Everything.

CHAPTER NINE

The shadows of the past

At eight in the evening the heat is still oppressive, so heavy it is almost tangible. He feels he could make good use of a fan when he gets out of his car in Piazza Gramsci, but it would clash somewhat with his inspectorial dignity. He starts walking, takes off his jacket and almost goes back to leave it in the car, but then he changes his mind, folds it and carries it over his shoulder with two fingers hooked under the collar – a bit uncomfortable. Fortunately he does not have far to go to reach Via Roma, and just as he is thinking this he sees the place there in front of him. A small garden without a gate, a building that used to be a primary school – two or three steps, no bell, but a big, pretentious plaque with two lines printed on it:

TOURISM ASSOCIATION
GUIGLIA TOURIST OFFICE

He knocks and waits, then pushes the door slightly, realizes it is open and walks in because all the lights are on.

At first sight it looks more like a private apartment than an office. In a spacious room there is a sparkling chandelier, a television that is switched off, a desk with a lamp and then another room – the library certainly, because he can see the bookshelves through the open door. Cataldo notices these things then transfers his attention to the man who stood up on seeing him come in and has walked round the desk to where he is standing now, just two metres away.

''Evening.' He looks at Cataldo with curiosity, and then adds, 'Please come in.'

'Thank you.'

'Can I help you? Are you looking for a book... a newspaper?'

'Not really.' And Cataldo smiles as the other man tries to guess.

'Are you doing some research?'

'No. Let's say I was searching for you.' And since the other man is evidently surprised he adds, 'You must be Nunzio, right?'

'Yes, but...'

'You don't understand. That makes sense. In fact, I'm sorry... I haven't introduced myself. Cataldo, Detective Inspector.' And he pulls out his badge, as he always does, and shows it to him. 'I'd like to have a word with you.'

'With me?'

'Yes, just a few questions...' he says, proceeding into the room while the other, slightly worried, walks backwards, '... about something that happened many years ago. But don't worry... you're not involved. It's just that you might be able to help me. In fact, you're the only one who might be able to help me.'

Perhaps he is flattered, perhaps it is just innate curiosity. In any case, Nunzio's attitude changes immediately. He is relaxed and willing now: 'I understand... but please take a seat.'

He points to the chair in front of the desk and then moves to sit in the chair on the other side, opposite Cataldo, and he switches the lamp on, almost as though he can't see very well in all that light.

'I wasn't sure you'd be open,' says Cataldo, to get things going.

'Indeed,' Nunzio confirms. 'I'm only open three evenings a

week – Monday, Wednesday, Friday, from nine o'clock. And that's only really for the few tourists that are around. In June there's hardly anyone.'

'Not many customers then?'

'No. And yet we have a good collection of books here – local history, folklore, traditions... from all over the Apennines, not just Guiglia. People used to come even from other towns, people working on dissertations. We've even got a few antique editions, or at least very rare ones...'

'But now no one comes?'

'Not often. At the most someone turns up looking for a thriller...'

Cataldo feels like laughing, but he does not want to lose his concentration now. So he leans over the desk and puts his hands together at the fingertips.

'That's not what I'm looking for,' he smiles, looking into his eyes. 'I'm here, let's say, to find some news about an event in the past. A graduation party, to be precise. Eighteen years ago.'

'Go on.'

'A small article about it appeared in *Guiglia Oggi*, or at least I think it did.'

Nunzio does not understand, but he looks interested.

'Who was the graduate?'

'Professor Ramondini.'

'And did it take place here in Guiglia?'

'The supper? It was nearby, at the Tre Lune restaurant.'

Cataldo leans back with his ankle on his knee, pressing his shin against the desk. Nunzio scratches his earlobe.

'I don't remember, but if you know the date...'

'21 February 1980.'

'That's no problem then. We have a complete set of *Guiglia*

Oggi. I keep the older ones at my house, because there isn't much space here.' He opens his arms and looks around. 'Just these two rooms, though they're quite big. I only keep more recent years on the shelves...'

'And you're sure you have 1980?'

'Oh yes, bound in a book. I just have to pull it out and bring it here. It's no problem,' he repeats. Then he pushes his chair back and scratches his head, almost as though to encourage the development of an idea. And then, after a second or two: 'I'm certain. It'll be in the attic. That's where it is, the year you're looking for.' He opens a drawer and pulls out a sheet of paper and a pencil. 'February 1980 you said?'

'Yes, 21 February.'

'The actual day isn't important. The magazine was quarterly or thereabouts...' He winks in complicity. 'It's always been run by volunteers like me, from the Tourist Office. Unpaid work, of course. But some of the articles were really very good...'

'I understand. And now?'

'Now?'

'Does *Guiglia Oggi* still exist? Is it still going?'

'*Guiglia Oggi?* Oh yes, though it's not the same as it used to be. It's more technical now, a sort of bulletin... with announcements from the mayor, the minutes of council meetings, etc.'

'And don't you work on it anymore?'

'That's right. I used to be an editor, I used to write pieces, take photographs. But now I spend most of my time in this office, not on the paper. It suits me better here – I open up, lend a few books... I'm more useful here, as a volunteer of course...'

'Of course, as a volunteer. What did you do before,

Nunzio?'

He has asked him suddenly, as though just wondering, with that affable concern that can appear to be both simple human interest and a search for familiarity.

'I was a clerk for the council. All my working life. First at Vignola, then here in Guiglia.'

'But you're not from around here, are you?'

'That's true. Can you still hear that?'

'From your accent?' He shakes his head. 'No, it's your name.'

'Nunzio? True. Nunzio Napolitano.' He pronounces it slowly, almost spelling it out.

'I'm from the south... a *maruchèin*.'

He has used the local dialect word, a corruption of 'Moroccan', and as he laughs he shows off his white teeth, as big as piano keys. One of them has a gold crown.

Cataldo smiles too: 'People have used that word to describe me too, you know. Countless times. But you get used to it. Or at least I did...'

'Right. People here aren't nasty. And I came here as young boy. I went to middle school here. I've been here almost all my life...'

And since Cataldo nods, he takes this as encouragement and continues: 'I don't know about you, but I'm from Cimitile. Province of Naples...'

'I'm from Catania, Sicily,' says Cataldo.

'It's a nice place, Cimitile, but no one's heard of it. I bet you haven't either. Look...'

He moves forward and reaches out towards a heavy ornament sitting to his right, on top of the desk. It is a model of a belltower, and it looks as though it is silver, but it must be plated, thinks Cataldo.

'Do you know what this is? No? It's the belltower of my town. But not the belltower that's there today... that one's a modern thing and is completely anonymous. This is the old Paleochristian one... perhaps the very first one in all Christendom, according to local tradition.'

'Ah. So it's a souvenir...'

'Yes. And it looks good here too.'

Cataldo picks it up, out of courtesy. He is right. It is solid, with a heavy pedestal – an excellent paperweight. Then he puts it back where it was, on the desk, and makes a pyramid with his hands on which he rests his chin.

'Listen. You said before that you used to take the photographs. Is it possible that you took the pictures in 1980, at Ramondini's supper?'

'At the restaurant? Well... I really don't remember... why? Are you sure someone took pictures?'

'Not sure. But it's possible.'

'We'll see when we get hold of the article. Who knows...'

He starts thinking, searching through his memory. And Cataldo observes him calmly. He is a tall man, bony, about sixty years of age with grey hair and glasses. An ordinary man, the type of man who does not stick in your mind. But there is that mark, on his nose. A big, ugly sore or wart.

'No, I just don't remember.' And then he smiles. 'So, if photos were taken, I don't think it was me who did the job.'

'Alright,' says Cataldo.

But he cannot take his eyes from his nose and Nunzio realizes.

'You've noticed that. It's a burn. Did it this morning when I was lighting the gas ring – the tip of a match flew off and hit me just here.' He touches the place on his nose.

'It's a shame because it looks really bad.'

98

'Let's just say it stands out.'

A few seconds of silence follow, and within himself Cataldo corrects the impression he had formed that it was a wart of some kind. Then Nunzio speaks: 'Come back tomorrow evening for the article. Is that alright, or is it too late?'

'No, that's fine.' He stops, however, and thinks. 'But tomorrow is Thursday, I don't want you to have to open up just for me...'

'It's no problem. One extra evening, just for an hour or so. Do come. Shall we say at nine o'clock?'

Cataldo thanks him, shakes his hand. And while he is saying goodbye he feels he has resolved something, at least for the moment. But outside, in the half-light, he suddenly presses the knuckles of one hand into the palm of the other until they are white. And he wonders how long it will last, this feeling of impotence. Of waiting.

He has stopped off at the Michelangelo, even though he is not really hungry. It is the heat, he says to himself, almost as though realizing only now. But then he thinks how strange this is, because it was even hotter in Catania and he really ought to be used to it, but maybe it is a different type of heat. He orders some plain spaghetti, some ham and a large glass of Lambrusco. For a moment he had been tempted to order the heavier *tigelle* and *borlenghi*, which he knows is the house special, but then he had decided they might be too much and abandons the idea. The food comes quickly because there are not many people in the place and so he starts eating, without enthusiasm, and he fills his glass. It is all good, it's just that he has no appetite. And he cannot get rid of those insistent, clear and annoying thoughts that have been with him all morning. And yet at home, even during his last leave, it was different. With his mother there cooking and serving for a start: cannelloni or *caponata*, *pasta alla Norma*, or *pasta con le sarde*. And the fish... here it's all frozen, while down there, so close to the sea: marinated shrimps, octopus in wine, swordfish carpaccio, his favourite. And then the barbecues with the neighbours, on the beach...

Of course, once or twice he had eaten well in Modena. Once or twice, he could not deny that. There had been that Sunday at Muliere's place, with his wife and kids. Tortellini with cream, *cotechino* and mashed potato and Barozzi cake. But how could Muliere compete with the sweets and ice-creams of Catania? You could not find anything as good as that if you did the rounds of this whole province. *Spumone... cannoli*, the sorbets, the *cassata*... there was never any need to watch his weight here in Modena and he always had to tighten his belt by a notch or two.

He continues chewing, but he is more thirsty than he is hungry and the quarter litre is almost finished. Even the wine is completely different. Personally he quite likes Lambrusco, of course, but it is almost like a soft drink when you taste it, compared to his own wines. Sometimes, towards the end of the summer, he had a real craving for something with more body, more of a man's wine. A red from Randazzo, for example, or Riposto, or the Ciclopi, with their strong, lively and full body...

He looks at the red remaining in the green glass and finds himself wondering what made him move up here. A friend who had mentioned the job opportunities? Or Schininà's son? But he was a salesman, travelling through, coming and going as he pleased – that was different. And all things considered such thoughts did not change anything. He was the one who had chosen to say farewell. Farewell to the silence of Sundays, to the August sun, to the trips in the country through the lemon groves, the lanes and the dry-stone walls leading down to the sea. Farewell to the siesta after lunch, to visiting the relatives. And farewell to her too.

None of this makes much sense. Not that it necessarily has to make sense. You cannot give life any other sense than actually living it. But when he stands up he can feel the nostalgia rising in his throat.

CHAPTER TEN

The invalid

Guiglia after suppertime. A neat town, with not many
lights on, even in June. The silence is opaque and soft, apart
from a moped now and then. The roads are hues of violet
and leaden grey. There is silence even beyond the centre,
here where Cataldo is driving. There is a row of terraced
houses, with low gates and balconies above the entrance
doors. Each home, strangely, is a slightly different colour
from the others – pastel shades that bring the sea to mind,
Liguria perhaps. But time has already turned them a little
grey.

The road is deserted, all that is on it are the residents' cars,
parked in rows out front. Cataldo drives to the very end, till
he reaches some land earmarked for more building, then he
turns back slowly, looking at the house numbers, looking
for the number he has in his head. At number 15 the bell is
just to the left of the gate and under it is a metal-framed slit
for the mail. He turns off the engine, looks at his watch,
makes up his mind as he gets out of the car and then rings.
For a second he stands there waiting, hands in pockets. Then
he hears the voice through the door.

'Who's there?'

'Police.'

The door opens slightly, a chain reflects the light. Cataldo
makes out a pale face, halfway up the door. He shows his
badge and waits in silence. The door almost closes, the chain
is taken off.

'Come in.'

The man who lets him in does everything on his own – wheels the chair by himself. He is about forty, looks older due to his disability, his grey hair and the bags under his eyes. But the eyes are certainly not those of an old man. Two bright, sharp lively eyes, thinks Cataldo. Disturbing in their intelligence.

'I'm sorry to bother you at this time of day. But it'll only take a few minutes...'

'That's not the problem. I've got plenty of time, as you can imagine. It's just that I don't understand why...'

'Ah... the reason? Well, it's not so difficult to imagine. Dr Zoboli's death...'

'Yes, but it was suicide...'

Cataldo does not stop. 'And I'm doing the rounds of all his friends. Just to get an idea... about him, his character. We always do this, when we investigate... suicide or not.'

'I see. But we weren't really friends.'

'Maybe not now, but you once were. At least back at school you were. In the same class – B – isn't that right?'

'Yes, but...'

'And perhaps you were friends even after. I mean, once you'd finished school...'

Cataldo pauses now and observes. Calabrese looks uneasy at the idea of continuing the conversation. And Cataldo is careful not to help him in any way, conscious that this silence gives him more time to scrutinize, to place him in his environment. Looking beyond him, through into the living room, he sees a glass next to an armchair and a book, its pages open, waiting to be read.

'Friends to the extent that, when Ramondini graduated, you all celebrated together. You, Zoboli, Miriam, Zanetti and Katia... with Don Lodi of course. Remember?'

'Yes, I remember, but that doesn't mean anything...' He lowers his voice, seems to start thinking. 'So many years have gone by...'

'Eighteen.'

'That many years? Anyway... yes, I remember.'

'Why?'

'Because I was surprised that he invited me. We studied different subjects at university... we'd lost touch. And I'd also lost touch with Zoboli and Miriam – the intellectuals...' He says it in a strange way, almost sarcastic. 'And Ramondini was older than me, we weren't in the same year at school...'

They have moved slowly into the living room and Calabrese invites Cataldo to sit, which he does on a chair at one end of the fine walnut table. The house is clean and tidy, he thinks, as he listens to the invalid's voice:

'That's why I was surprised.'

'And flattered?'

'Well... yes. It was a chance to start the friendship again. We'd all studied together, right up to the end of school... we'd shared many things at an impressionable age, things you don't forget easily.'

'Why did you call them the intellectuals?'

'Those two? Because it's the truth. They were very pretentious, perhaps because they were good at literature – they started lecturing and they never stopped. Him especially, he was very much admired... with all the books he'd read and all the things he knew. He was the best at school, you can ask Don Lodi about that...'

'And yet at Ramondini's party everyone felt sorry for him.'

'Ah... yes.' He smiles, but in an almost melancholy way. 'They've told you about that? It's true, he started drinking, and he never usually did. That's why I remember it. At the end of the evening he could barely stand...'

'And he drove home in that state?'

'Of course not. Miriam took him home. I don't know when, exactly, but before the party finished. Yes, a bit before that.'

'And she drove?'

'No doubt about that. It was dark too... winter.'

'So she did drive.' Then, as if to himself, 'But why did he drink so much?' And he looks at Calabrese, who purses his lips, and waits for a moment before speaking.

'Sometimes you drink to forget. Or out of envy.'

'You think so?'

'I don't think so. I've heard people say it.'

'Ah... let's see if I can guess.' He crosses his legs and pretends to think, but in truth he already has an idea. 'Usually people envy other people's success, no?' And he stares at him. 'Ramondini?'

He nods. 'A brilliant graduation, the beginning of a brilliant career...'

'All his own work?'

Calabrese opens his mouth, then he closes it, embarrassed, before muttering, 'That's not for me to say.'

'Or you don't want to say. Let's just leave it then. So Zoboli was a bit envious of Ramondini...'

'But it should have been the other way round.'

'Just a minute, I don't understand. Why should Ramondini have envied Zoboli?'

'Plenty of reasons.'

'Give me just one.'

'For example... his success with women.'

'Are you thinking of Miriam?'

105

'Well... yes. But not only her...'

'And Ramondini?' But Calabrese looks uneasy, so he adds, 'No women? Just books and research?'

'That's the way it was. He'd never had a girlfriend, a love affair, that we knew of... apparently he was still a virgin.' He says this quickly, blushing.

'Oh really?' Cataldo says. 'But apart from this, he was interested in women?' And for a moment he is undecided whether to speak clearly and to touch two fingers to his earlobe.

'Don Lodi was the only person he was interested in.'

There is a moment's silence. Calabrese, embarrassed, purses his lips again, and his cheeks are bright red. Cataldo thinks it odd that he should know so much, about everyone – a man who spends all his time at home, in a wheelchair.

'You spoke about envy before... do people envy you?'

'Me? For what?'

'For your money, for example.'

'Money, yes...' and he smiles. 'But who'd really envy me, Inspector? Have you taken a good look? Here, on my own all the time. Not even a nurse, or a cleaning lady...'

'You don't have one?'

'No.'

'Well... there are worse things. The more thoughts crowd your mind, the more solitude becomes a refuge. Almost necessary...'

'You're wrong. No one is happy to be alone. All the questions crop up, all the doubts you have inside. And you come to realize what a void you live in. Because we're all full of nothing.' But these last words are said under his breath, almost as though to himself.

Cataldo looks around. The conversation is beginning to

depress him. Because in the other man's manner – unexpressed, suffocated – there is a shade of malice or spite that is strangely disquieting. And in his eyes, at moments, there is an unhealthy expression, as though he had never managed to rid himself of some resentment, or as though he really did live on fragments of other peoples' lives.

'Who might have wanted to kill Zoboli?' he asks suddenly, in the silence.

'But didn't he commit suicide?'

'Yes, I'm just suggesting. If it weren't suicide...'

'Have you completed your enquiries?'

'Almost. It won't be long now.'

'I see.' And he thinks for a moment, 'Well, if he didn't kill himself... this is just a hypothesis, of course...'

'Of course.'

'Well... it could have been someone's husband... someone who'd been betrayed, I mean...' He was about say a *cornuto*, a cuckold with his horns, but that was too facile.

'Or?'

'Or... that guy from Turin, what's his name... Marchisio, I think. There's no one else I can think of...'

'How do you know about him?'

'Everyone knows, Inspector. He arrived on Monday, started nosing around, asking questions... it's a small town, Guiglia.'

He decides not to ask who told him, which of the people he has already interviewed... he would only reply that he had heard it mentioned.

'You know who he is, of course...'

'I know everything, yes.'

'You don't think there could be, let's say, professional motives behind all this?'

'I don't know. It's not my world, I told you.'

'I ask you that because of the envy. Between him and Ramondini, you mentioned that...'

'I did, but when I think about it I don't see it as a strong enough motive. Even though I don't know the university world, research... the way it works...'

'And the working relationships?'

'Exactly.'

'Alright.' Cataldo sighs and then: 'Let's talk now about something you do know well. Tecnodomus. There are two partners... you and Zanetti. Is that right?'

'Yes.'

'Equal partners?'

'Fifty-fifty.'

'Okay. When did you buy into the business?'

'In which year? 1983.'

'Three years later,' says Cataldo, under his breath.

'Sorry?'

'Nothing. I was just thinking... and tell me, buying into Tecnodomus must have cost a bit...'

'That's true.'

'I don't want to know how much, that doesn't interest me... and I'm not thinking about you, because you're rich...' and he smiles as Calabrese lifts his hand to deny the fact. 'No... everyone here says so. Rather I was thinking about where Zanetti found the money. He doesn't seem to be rich, and no one has said he is...'

Calabrese gestures agreement. 'Actually it was a surprise for me too, and yet that's what happened. He played football for two years, for Modena and he even had a trial for Bologna, who at that time were in the first division... but he certainly didn't make his money in football. Everyone knows that...'

'And this absolves you from all possible lack of discretion.'

Calabrese nods, seeming to appreciate Cataldo's understanding.

'But it's certainly a bit of a mystery,' Cataldo continues. 'I visited his house today. It doesn't look to me as though he's filthy rich...'

'Did you see Katia as well?' asks Calabrese suddenly.

'Of course.'

'Was she on her own?'

'Yes. Why?'

'Nothing. I just wondered.'

But Calabrese is confused, ill at ease. And Cataldo has an idea, which he decides to pursue.

'What do you think of Zanetti?'

'We've been friends for many years... we even sat together at school.'

'And as a man?'

'He's a lucky man... yes, he's been lucky in life.'

'And Katia?'

'Sorry?'

'Is she your friend too?'

'Do you think,' and the ironic vein in his voice is, all things considered, respectful, 'that this is of any importance?'

'Do you?' is Cataldo's response, in exactly the same tone. And since Calabrese says nothing: 'So, is she your friend?'

He seems to look through Cataldo, then he moves his head slightly and lifts his hand to his mouth. Cataldo does not rush him because he already understands.

'You're in love with her, aren't you?' he says, almost whispering. 'Ever since your schooldays?'

He nods yes, as though ashamed. Then he whispers: 'We

have no control over the duration of a love, just as we have no control over the duration of our lives.'

'I know who said that. But those who have only dreamed of love cannot talk of it.'

'Why?'

'Because in the end we only know what we are, or what we live.'

'That may be.' And he looks at Cataldo now in a different way, with a note of irritation. 'You might be right. But remember one thing. For those who are patient, not every wait is a defeat.'

It rings almost like a judgement and Cataldo is about to ask him what he means, when the telephone in the entrance rings. Calabrese goes to answer, turning the wheels of the chair and soon Cataldo hears him say, 'Hello?' Then the voice is lowered immediately so he cannot hear from the living room. Cataldo gets up and moves towards him, moves past him, opens the door and waves goodbye. Calabrese stops talking, covers the receiver with his hand and says:

'Nothing else, Inspector?'

'Not for now, no. If I need to, I'll be back.'

And as he walks towards the car, Cataldo thinks it is a shame he has no idea to whom Calabrese is speaking, and that it is the second time in the last few hours that he has had that regret. The phone. It's always the phone. And then in the silence, his hand in his pocket to look for the key, he is not surprised by the ringing of his own mobile as it interrupts his thoughts. And in the warm evening he hears the voice of Arletti, the medical examiner, loud and clear as though he were standing there. It is the post-mortem: it is ready, but they had best talk about it face to face. Tomorrow morning at ten o'clock, in Modena, in the coroner's office. It is urgent. Cataldo agrees.

He starts the engine and feels more relieved, without any real reason. He is just waiting for some new fact, something to provide the impetus that will help get past this moment of stasis, of inertia. And before he pulls away he takes another look at the house, at the window, the light behind the glass, the curtains closed. And there is Calabrese's face, watching him, with a grin. Or rather, a strange, angry grimace.

CHAPTER ELEVEN

Some certainty

Now he wants to get a move on, to avoid the heat that is already building up. At nine in the morning the sun scorches the car upholstery and glares brightly as it reflects off the house windows. In the garden of a villa he is parked next to, there is a girl on a deckchair, soaking up the sun with her eyes closed, as if she were at the seaside.

As if she were at the seaside, yes. The sea at Catania, from the road, the sea just beyond the beach. And this vision conjures up images, gestures. Sudden flashes in his memory. Who knows how long they had been building up inside.

They had walked higher up on the sand, because the sea was a little rough and waves were occasionally breaking higher up the beach, towards them. That was the last time, on the seafront at Ognina. Then they had gone out on the jetty, to talk. Below them the tide dragged slowly on the green stones and strands of seaweed fluttered just below the surface. The day was coming to an end, and with the setting of the sun the warmth was dissipating too. They were moving into the coolness and the calm of autumn. The moon alone gave a warm light, almost a summer light...

Last summer, one year ago, near Acireale. There before them were some rocks that looked like ruined walls, rising out of a sea so blue and calm it seemed solid. No trace of wind at all, just a seagull, in silence, which completed a long glide over a boat before resting on its prow, like a figurehead. Why had that remained in his head?

He shakes himself, looks at the road. And now a sense of

fatigue comes over him, as though the flow of life had suddenly stopped. And he, too, wants to stop, to close his eyes in all that light. Just like the girl sunbathing. Perhaps she is even beautiful, who knows?

It is even warmer in Modena. Arletti seems to be feeling it too, despite the white linen suit, the same one he was wearing yesterday. His hand is damp when he shakes Cataldo's and from close up Cataldo sees there are two or three drops of sweat on his forehead. There is another man there and Arletti introduces them to each other, surprised that Cataldo already knows him.

'Dr Zironi, from forensics...'

'Ciao, Luca. How goes it?'

'Same as ever. Work.'

'You've been dragged into this too, then?'

'I'm helping out.'

He is a small, bony man, older than Cataldo and with the bad-tempered look of someone chronically ill with cynicism and indigestion.

'So, colleagues,' begins Arletti, as he always does, 'we have the preliminary results of the post-mortem. Time of death between nine and ten o'clock on the evening of Tuesday 23, as I had predicted... remember?'

'Of course.'

'Straight line of fire, close contact entry wound to the right temple, slit-like exit wound to the left occipital wall. The contact shot can be seen from the burnt skin around the first wound. Bullet travelled through the skull completely – instant death, etc. etc. But you already knew all that.'

'Quite,' says Cataldo.

'But now comes the real surprise, and it's best if he tells

you about it.'

So Cataldo turns to the small man who clears his throat and he knows he is about to say something important and will say it in very few words.

'It wasn't suicide.'

'No?'

'No.' And he pauses, almost as though savouring the shock. 'Ballistic examination of the pistol confirms it.'

'Tell me.'

'The Beretta next to the dead man really was his and it had been used to fire a shot.' Another pause. 'But the bullet we found in the room doesn't match.'

Cataldo would like to ask if he is sure, but he knows that Zironi will let him know. In the meantime he rubs his nose with two fingers, as he always does when he suddenly has to think about something.

'I mean, it doesn't match the striations, the linear grooves produced by the barrel. You know how we do this, don't you? We fired the Beretta into a soft target, recovered the bullets and compared the grooves with the grooves on the one in the room...'

'And they don't match?'

'Not at all.'

'Incontrovertible proof.'

'That's right. No two ways about it. The barrel striations are like an identity card for a pistol. And with the electron microscope there's no margin of error at all...'

Now Zironi looks at Arletti, who nods. 'And then there are two other things.'

'Yes?'

'In a suicide the direction of the bullet track is usually oblique. I mean, from below upwards, when people shoot themselves in the head...'

'Right. Here it's the other way round... and the other thing?'

'The other thing is that there is always some soot, or non-combusted residue on the hand that holds the gun... on the palm, on the back of the hand, on the forearm...'

'And the dead man?'

'Nothing.'

'So it's murder.'

'Exactly.'

Cataldo looks at Zironi, thinks for a moment, then decides. 'So what do you think happened?'

Zironi likes the question, which promotes him from being a technician to being an interpreter of the mystery. 'Well, okay... it could have gone like this: the murderer must have had a Beretta just like the victim's and he entered easily because the victim opened the door for him. I was told there were no signs of forced entry, right?'

'That's right.'

'So he was either a friend, or he wasn't but they had an appointment. Once inside he shot the victim in the temple while Zoboli was sitting down, standing by his side, as the doctor mentioned...'

Arletti confirms with a nod of his head.

'And then?'

'Then he took the dead man's pistol from somewhere and put it on the desk, near his head... using gloves, of course, having fired a shot with the pistol, who knows where. Maybe out of the window...'

'That's possible,' says Cataldo, evidently thinking it through. 'An isolated house, his wife away... perhaps even the television on. Few people if anybody at all would have heard the shots...'

'And then he wiped the prints off, if he'd actually left any that is. If he wasn't using gloves right from the beginning.'

'Unlikely, with this heat. And in that case Zoboli would have been suspicious from the moment he let him in... by the way, any news on the fingerprints?'

'Not really. Only the victim's on the Beretta, but if the murderer used gloves that makes sense. In the entrance though... just a minute... to be precise, on the light switch and on the wall, just a few centimetres away, there were prints from someone else. But who knows how long they'd been there, and who they belong to.'

'Are they clear prints?'

'Some of them, yes, they're visible. Others are superimposed and rather mixed up.'

'I see. Thanks.'

He has been efficient and very precise. As always.

'Do you have any other questions?'

'One. Has anything ever stumped you?'

His lips trace a slight smile on his face: 'Yes, once. In my second year at primary school.'

'I would have bet on that.'

In the silence the doctor's dry laugh rings out.

Cataldo drives slowly on his way back to Guiglia. And in the meantime he thinks, with the radio off. The hole in the wrong temple leads him to think it was someone Zoboli did not know, someone who had no idea Zoboli was left-handed. Indeed, someone like Marchisio. But at least two things do not add up. Firstly, a stranger, turning up whether unannounced or by appointment, could not have known that Zoboli owned a Beretta 7.65, necessary information to go there with an identical pistol and organize the whole setup. No, he could not have done that. But it was worthwhile testing something out.

Marchisio again, in front of him in the small room that looks out on the courtyard, the same room in which he had spoken with the owner. Every now and then the muffled noises of the hotel come to them – tables being laid for lunch. How many times has Cataldo gone through this performance – feigning irritation, loading his voice, looking straight in the eye, all just to make the trick plausible?

'Any questions, Inspector?'

'Just one. Why did you lie to me?'

'Me? When?'

'When you told me you'd never been to Zoboli's house.'

'But it's true. I told you that because it's true.'

'You did visit him.'

'Who says so?'

'A witness.' He stares. 'A reliable witness, who lives opposite Zoboli, on the other side of the road.'

There is a bit of unease in his voice when he replies, but it lasts just an instant:

'And you pull this witness out now?'

'I'm not pulling him out. He's come forward now of his own free will. And do you want to know what he saw? Either way, I'm going to tell you.' The tone of his voice becomes harder, firmer. 'He saw you go through the gate after nine o'clock.'

'The timekeeping's a bit vague. After nine?'

'Yes.'

'Which, surprise surprise, will also be the time of death... you know, this sounds like a bluff to me.' He stands up, takes a newspaper from the table, indifferent. But Cataldo sees that he is faking it.

'It's no bluff, believe me. And there's a way for you to get out of this. Are you prepared to give me your fingerprints, to compare them with the prints found in the villa?'

'Found where in the villa?'

'Well, let's see... in the entrance, for example... on the light switch.'

'Prints, eh?' And he looks at his hands. 'When?'

'Immediately... it's in your own best interests.' And since he hesitates: 'You've never been in there, right? So you've got nothing to be afraid of. I repeat, it really is in your own best interests...'

Marchisio's fingers fidget nervously, creasing the newspaper. Cataldo waits, because the job is almost done.

'You're right. I went there.' His voice is an embarrassed murmur now.

'And why didn't you tell me straight away?'

'Fear. I was scared because...'

'It doesn't matter now, just carry on.'

'I met him on Tuesday afternoon, I told him I was writing a book on a topic he knows about. I asked him for advice, information.'

'And what did he say?'

'He was kind right from the start. He said he had time, that his wife was away and he could help me immediately. So he gave me an appointment for nine thirty.' He looks at Cataldo before adding: 'I know what you're thinking. No, he didn't recognize me. I'm sure.'

'Or at least you think he didn't. And then?'

'I arrived on time, and you can imagine all the rest. The gate was open, the door was ajar, the light was off...'

'Just like in a thriller.'

Marchisio ignores the irony: 'I switched the light on, I looked around a bit and then I found him. Dead. I got scared then...'

'Of what?'

'Of an ambush, a trap... of being set up. Just like all those years ago. And so I ran away. Don't you understand?'

'Just calm down now.'

He had raised his tone for a moment, but Cataldo's voice reminds him that they are not alone, and brings him back to a minimum of courtesy.

'I'm sorry,' he whispers. 'But it's the truth. I swear it's the truth.'

'Just like when you swore you'd never been in there...'

Marchisio says nothing, his ears bright red. But within himself Cataldo knows that it all might just be true. He knows that a man who lives in fear does not change over the years, even years spent in jail.

'You can go. I've finished.'

Marchisio gets up and heads for the door. Then he turns, almost as though he wants to say something, but he says nothing. He leaves the door open. Cataldo moves to close it.

CHAPTER TWELVE

Fear

They wait in silence, all three of them, and they have no idea why he has asked them to come. That is why they are so tense, embarrassed. During the wait, feeling uneasy, they sit down after a while and now they look at each other furtively, lowering their eyes when they meet another's gaze. Miriam and Katia are sitting at the table, close to each other, but without touching. Miriam's head is bowed, completely motionless. Ramondini from the very beginning chooses to stand near a window, his hand on the glass, as though looking for some support. Then, perhaps a bit surprised not to have noticed it before, he starts looking at a copy of a famous oil painting: Dalì's *Les Quatre Elephants*, hanging near the door. In the end he sits too, the last to do so. The splendour of the bookshelves, with the warm oak and the ivory of the books, the stuccoes and the inlay, and the cool half-light in contrast with the muggy heat outside, at once both assuages and exacerbates the fear they all feel.

Ramondini is the most visibly afraid. He is slouched now in the honey-coloured leather armchair behind the desk. He holds his hands in his lap, and perhaps it is not fear, but just the afternoon heat that makes them sweaty and makes him wring them continuously. His eyes are fixed, no feeling in them, nothing. They do not change expression, not even when his lips force themselves into a smile. He controls his gaze, making his eyes run over the other people in the room, without ever letting himself catch their eye. But it does not take much to see that he is afraid.

120

'Why do you think he's asked us to come here?'

'Can't you guess?'

In the tangible tension that envelops them all, any attempt at making conversation drowns and silence returns. A silence thick with uncertainty, doubt. And suspicion.

After a while Don Lodi enters, and the women start to get up, but he gestures, telling them to remain seated because they will begin immediately. Only Ramondini insists, clumsily, and offers the armchair, the priest's usual place, while he takes a place halfway along the table, opposite the window. Don Lodi clears his voice and starts.

'To begin with, I thank you all for having come and I promise I won't steal much time. But it's important that we meet, given the situation...'

'Which means?' Katia's voice carries impatience, but Don Lodi pays no attention to the interruption and continues: 'I know that Inspector Cataldo, a very capable man, is doing the rounds of all of us. And he's asking each of us, myself included, about the others. Indeed, he started with me. And why? Because Zoboli took his own life? Evidently Cataldo doesn't believe this, and we have to know just how much we believe it as well.'

Miriam, red in the face, seems to want to say something, but she thinks again. The other two are rigid in their silence, not even looking at one another. It is as if this observation has illuminated a hypothesis that is as terrible as it has been unsaid up to now. 'So,' continues Don Lodi, his voice a little too controlled, trying to appear natural, 'I now wonder: why so many questions? Perhaps he's already sure it's murder and he feels that he has to look for a motive in Zoboli's character, in his life and among his friends? Or does he even think that one of us killed him?'

'But what are you saying? Are you mad?' Katia blurts out suddenly. Miriam meanwhile swallows, her eyes on the table.

'It's just an idea.'

'A stupid idea!'

'Katia!' The priest's reproof is more affectionate than severe. 'We must not fight. We have to keep calm and united.' He emits a conciliatory sigh. 'If I expressed myself badly, I apologise. I'm making hypotheses, no more than that...'

'But why? If it was suicide.'

'We don't know that yet... we can't know before the post-mortem results. And there's another thing.'

During the pause that follows there is a mixture of various emotions: curiosity, anguish, anxiety. But above all it is fear that dominates. Like a contagion, they pass it on from one to another. Miriam sits, diffident, on the edge of her chair; her face is taut and every now and then she passes her tongue over her lips. Katia is composed, elegant as usual. But Ramondini, who has already noticed the careful, perfectly applied makeup, wonders if it is a gesture of defiance or a small, admirable attempt to impose an illusion of normality on their group's apprehension.

'We know that this outsider... this Marchisio, has come back here after eighteen years... straight out of prison after serving time for Cristoni's death, a crime he has always maintained he had nothing to do with. So the fact is: why has he come back? To take revenge on us? And why on us? Well, there is an answer to this even though...'

He looks at them all, his eyes moving slowly, but no one speaks.

'Because he claims to have recognized Zoboli's face much later, when he was already in prison... says he saw Zoboli in the car that caused the accident... the car that then turned back while he was running away, and that it was Zoboli who took all that money...'

According to him...' says Katia, irony in her voice.

'Indeed, according to him Zoboli wasn't driving and it was midnight. And Miriam,' he stares at her, gestures towards her, 'remembers that she was driving, but it was an hour earlier...'

Miriam frowns and for a moment she looks almost ugly.

'It's true. Giulio was with me, I was driving. But it wasn't midnight, we left an hour earlier.'

'From my party, yes. It was my graduation celebration, remember?'

Ramondini is still sitting, with his gaze fixed on the green of the garden outside. It is the first time he has spoken and everyone turns to look at him, almost as though actually realizing in that moment that he is here too.

'It's true. I swear,' repeats Miriam obstinately and passionately. 'And his death can't have anything to do with that accident eighteen years ago!'

'I don't know,' says the priest quietly, as though following his own train of thought. 'Often the past is the key to the present. And everyone is responsible for his or her own past.'

And since they do not understand: 'I was thinking about Cataldo, and that graduation party. Did you know he's very interested in it? He's especially interested in certain pictures, taken by someone from the tourist office and then published in *Guiglia Oggi*.'

'It must have been Nunzio,' says Katia. 'He did everything at the paper. Doubtless Cataldo will have interviewed him already.'

'And what does he want with that photo? Checking up on who was there and who wasn't? Would that be of any use, after eighteen years?'

Don Lodi looks at the three one by one, as though inviting them to agree with what he is about to say: 'For this reason I advise you to keep calm, to remain united. Just like back in school, before the exams. Remember? There is no problem that cannot be solved, as long as there is good will and mutual trust. Or even mutual fear,' and he smiles, or at least tries to, 'but I hope we're not afraid.'

He breathes deeply, starts looking around again. Everyone's eyes follow his, except for Miriam's, which are fixed on a point on the table. No one speaks, however. And he surprises himself now, as he hears his own voice loud and clear in that silence: 'You'd all known Giulio for a long time, you were his friends. That's why I turn now to your consciences. I do not say this just for effect, believe me. If any of you knows something that might shed some light on his death, I beg you to speak. To confide in me. Now or in private, it makes no difference. But within our group first, then we speak to Cataldo. To keep quiet at this stage, as well as being an injustice could also be dangerous. Because...' he stops for a moment, then starts again, with complete calm: 'It doesn't matter, you know better than I do... I simply repeat: if anyone knows anything, recount it and as soon as possible.'

'But what can we possibly know about it! You've known us all our lives, haven't you? Or do you really think that one of us is responsible? If that's the way you see it, spit it out for God's sake!'

Ramondini has spoken impulsively, losing control of his nerves, turning abruptly towards the priest. But it was just a momentary loss of control, and he is already regretting it: 'Forgive me, Athos, I'm sorry. I'm very sorry... excuse me. I don't know what came over me. My God... you're right, we must stick together...' And since Don Lodi offers no reply, he adds, his voice cracking: 'You don't believe it was a crime, right? You don't really think Giulio was killed?'

The priest looks at him, his mouth covered with the palm of his hand. Then he replies slowly: 'I don't know. It's not a geometry problem... it's not a school test. It's not enough just to keep studying it to give it some logical sense...' And he almost seems to smile.

Miriam cannot stand it any more. First their hypocrisy, now these words. She stands up and shouts: 'Enough! Please, enough! He didn't kill himself, you all know that, even though none of you has the courage to say so!'

Don Lodi looks straight at her, and the others turn towards her as well, staring at her in consternation as she opens her mouth again, slowly, but says nothing, nothing to add to those words. For some moments, which seem to last an incredible length of time, she holds her breath, and her tears, but her face is strained and when she finally speaks again her voice has changed and is more confrontational: 'But aren't you ashamed? Do you really have to talk about his death as though it were a riddle, or a TV thriller? This is Giulio we're talking about! Giulio, not an outsider! He's dead and we're here talking, as though we couldn't care less.'

'And what are we supposed to do? Do you want us to shut up? Do you want us to pretend nothing's happened? In my opinion it makes sense to talk. He was my friend... had been for many years. And if I manage to keep calm, you can do it too, if you make the effort.'

Ramondini's face is ablaze after these words. And Miriam's laugh is as bitter as the tears she will not cry.

'You! A friend of his? You're the one who stole everything from him – the ideas, the notes! You made him work for nothing and then you came along and did him out of all the credit. First with Giulio, then with others, the same story... flattery, promises, the same old story. And remember that just as I know these things, many others know them as well... the truth behind your fine academic career!'

'And why should I have killed Giulio?' He replies. 'I really don't understand... to prevent all this rubbish becoming public knowledge? Instead it's you...'

'Me?'

'You're the one with a motive, and a much bigger motive than mine.'

'And what would that be?'

'It's the infidelity, isn't it? Your husband had a lover... don't tell me you didn't know that. Don't say that because no one here will believe you... And if it's true that you knew... well, there's nothing that sparks off hatred like a love betrayed.'

Suddenly the telephone rings. A diversion that interrupts the tension. Everyone turns towards Don Lodi, who gets up slowly, walks towards a small table and lifts the receiver.

'Yes, that's me.' Then he turns his back, lowers his voice and no one hears anything, not a single word, apart from 'I'm on my way,' or 'I'll come,' at the end of the call.

He hangs up and for a moment stands there near the telephone, looking at it as though it were something alive. Then he raises his eyes, sees everyone's quizzical look and for a moment almost seems to want to tell them who it was and what they wanted. But he does not. Instead he says: 'Good.

Our frankness has been bitter, even offensive. But it took great honesty for it to be that way. Because we all want the truth, whatever that may be. Only the truth. And now, excuse me...'

They all stand up at the same time without looking at one another. Because this is everything – they have already said enough. Then they follow him to the door, nodding good-bye, embarrassed. No shaking of hands.

At the door they turn to look at the priest. 'Everyone is responsible for his or her own past,' he repeats under his breath. And then, for them: 'If this affair isn't resolved soon, it's going to turn us all into much worse people.'

CHAPTER THIRTEEN

Another dead man

Nine in the evening of that same Thursday. On entering, gripping the door handle, the heartbeat quickens. And it is not only felt in the chest, but it resounds in the head, the eyes, the veins in the throat, in the wrists. Another second and it will be impossible to turn back. Pushing the door, moving into the room. Ears listen for a squeak from the door, trying not to feel the hammering of the heart in the temples, and the sound of breathing. The room is in half-light. The glass chandelier is switched off. The only light comes from the lamp on the desk. And from the television, its volume turned down, its colours flickering on the white walls. As though the place were closed to the public, or as though whoever is inside is not expecting a visit.

He appears suddenly from under the desk, red in the face. Evidently something had fallen, he had bent over to look for it and now he is back on his feet, believing himself to be alone – Nunzio screws his eyes up instinctively, then smiles, though surprised. He walks round from behind the desk. He is not wearing a jacket because of the heat.

'Hello! Do you need a book? One of ours?'

'Yes. But are you open?'

'No. That is, yes... don't worry.'

'Ah. Well... I'm looking for a history of Guiglia... the one by Rabetti, I think, the one written during the Second World War...'

'Yes, we've got that. But there's an even more recent one, if you're interested... by Don Gavioli. *Guiglia and its*

Ancient Marquisate,' he recites, confidently, almost with pride. 'I know because we published it, the tourist office.'

'Ah... that'll be fine. Thank you. I'll take that one.'

Two things seem striking. The sound of the voice – calm, confident, while the hands sweat and the knees shake. And then that wart on Nunzio's nose, right there on the tip – so big, standing out. It is strange, comes the thought, how in the midst of anxiety, one notices the smallest, the most insignificant things.

Nunzio smiles, satisfied. 'Just a minute... come with me.'

He moves towards the other room, turning his back in the process. And it all happens in an instant. There on the desk, open at the very page, is the purpose of this visit. Then a vision of Nunzio's back in the half-light, where a black Y shape indicates he is wearing a pair of braces. And now it has come... the moment.

The blow makes a sharp noise, like a bat hitting hard wood. A violent blow to the neck. But it is not accurate, not to the nape, which is what the trembling hand had sought to hit. Nunzio suddenly shifts sideways, crashing into the doorframe, then he falls to his knees, without understanding. And he holds his hand out in an instinctive gesture, like a vague plea, a silent invocation. The shadow halts, materializes above him. In one hand it holds something resembling a paperweight, which is then raised and lowered once again. Another crack, stronger than the first one, almost a dull smack. The blood gushes from the back of his neck now and the red flows over his white shirt. More blood comes from his mouth, forming just a line flowing from the corner of his mouth. Nunzio jerks, relaxes, then jerks again at the third blow. In his brain there is an explosion of white light, much stronger than any light bulb, a sunburst; and other blades of pain run through him, more flashes of light as he is there, face down, on the floor and he feels a warm liquid spreading underneath him. With extreme effort he lifts his head, as though trying to bring the presence above him into focus. But he cannot. Just one more flash of pain, a sense of fire. And the taste of his own blood on his tongue, between his lips. And his vision blurs. And an infinite tiredness, and no fear. 'Why?' he thinks, already in darkness.

The shadow breathes deeply and turns back to the desk. It knows what has to be done. The sound of the old paper being leafed through – like dry leaves. And then another sound – sharp, strident. And the hand goes to the pocket, clenched in a fist. That is it. Everything is done. No... the handkerchief, there, to remove, to wipe away... quickly, quicker... the prints. Time to go now, if possible – legs buckling, heart in mouth. At the threshold, for a moment that feels like a century, the breath is held. Then the shadow opens the door and waits for one more second before leaving. Hot air in the face, feels like the Sirocco. And sweat everywhere – across the forehead, down the back, under the clothes. Just keep moving, without running, towards the car parked nearby in Piazza Gramsci. As the car starts moving a dog barks far away. But no one comes to look.

It is twelve minutes past nine when Cataldo arrives. The slight delay is because of a phone call: he was already in his car when Petronio rang, wanting to know the latest developments. He has every right, of course, but with the whole day at his disposal, why at that time? Yup, that guy really knows how to be a pain in the backside. Now Cataldo is here crossing the garden, going up the steps. The door is closed but the handle turns. So he knocks softly, out of politeness, and then stands back to wait for Nunzio's voice to tell him to come in. Nothing but silence from inside. He knocks again. Silence. So he presses his nose against the glass – the television's rectangle of moving light illuminates the white walls with flashes and the lamp on the desk is on as well. Cataldo touches his nose for a second out of worry. Then he sighs and makes up his mind.

He pushes the door and enters. No movement, no sound, just the ticking of a clock somewhere. Strange, he thinks, that he had not heard it first time. But now he smells something too – the sweetish smell of blood, before he sees it. Now, slowly, his senses primed, he walks backwards towards the door, feels the wall, finds the switch and turns on the big light.

There between the two rooms, face down, is the body – arms and legs slightly askew, the head smashed. All around him on the floor there is blood, so much blood. There is even blood on the doorframe, on the books low down on the first shelf and even some distance away from the body – drops of dark blood that has not yet clotted. Cataldo suddenly thinks that he would never have imagined Nunzio had so much blood in him. He moves closer, puts a hand under the chin and gently lifts. It is enough just to have a swift impression of Nunzio's face – his lips pulled back in a grimace – to realize that what he sees is a massive cranial fracture, with the blood darkening, clotting. He cannot look any more and he lets the head fall before turning back, towards the desk, but at the same moment he remembers there is no phone up here. With a sigh he pulls out his mobile, but waits for a moment, looks around, before going outside to call. And he tries to let his gaze soak up every detail in the room. Because no detective, even the sharpest, ever knows right from the very beginning which are the essential pieces of information: information that may disappear, if it is not noted immediately, at the very beginning.

And on the desk is the purpose of his visit. To one side, stained red, is the Cimitile belltower. It is there on a sheet of headed paper and the blood has flowed in little streams over it, almost obliterating the address of the tourist office. And there, in the very centre of the desk, is a heavy, bound volume: *Guiglia Oggi* from 1980 and it is open – it is the one he has come to see. And he understands that Nunzio has kept his word, kept his promise. His last promise.

He holds his breath as he leans over the pages with just a little hope and with much fear. He realizes almost immediately that the page he is looking for simply is not there. He checks twice, carefully, as the tension rises – the date, the page numbers. Pages three and four are missing. So he folds the compact block of pages backwards towards the point where the binder stitched them, looking for proof of the fact that the page has been cut out. But it has not been cut with a knife or a razor blade – no, it has been ripped out. With the naked eye you can see some residue of paper, there where the edge of the page is still held by the stitching. A job done hastily, anxiously, by someone who beat him to it. By just a few minutes.

And now the anger rises, making him almost nauseous. He turns to look at Nunzio, moves closer and leans over him. From Cataldo's throat, involuntarily, there comes a furious, agonized sound. Then he closes his eyes and shakes his head vigorously, two or three times, not wanting to believe it. All the cruelty, the injustice, of that death. An old man, with a book in his hand, suddenly appears behind him. 'What's happening?' He moves forward, looks at Cataldo, then at the body on the floor. 'Oh my God!' he says in one breath.

Cataldo takes him by the arm, moves outside and makes a telephone call. The first to arrive is a doctor, the first they could find and he is a tourist, here in Guiglia on holiday. A small, balding man with a nicotine-stained moustache who, clearly uneasy, does what he can around the dead man. Cataldo waits until he is finished and in the meantime the others arrive and then he waits until the body is covered with a rubberized sheet and is carried away by a guy from the mortuary – who knows how and where they managed to get hold of him at this time, at eleven o'clock. Then he decides that is enough.

Only a couple of hours have gone by when he leaves, and already photographers and journalists from two local television stations have arrived. One guy shouts something in the warm evening and immediately there are three of them running after Cataldo – two women and a man, shoving microphones in his face and shooting questions at him. But he says nothing – not one single idea, not one supposition. Because he knows well that when the media get hold of ideas, they immediately transform them into facts, and he does not want that. Twenty metres back towards the door, two men in shirtsleeves have video cameras on their shoulders, pointed at anyone who leaves the tourist office. Tomorrow morning, or maybe even tonight, the whole town will know.

CHAPTER FOURTEEN

Certain memories

He has slept very little, woke up early when it was still dark. A bitter taste in his mouth. He well knows it is partly due to the heat, partly due to Nunzio. And now he is here, thinking – lying on his bed, his eyes gazing at the ceiling as his chest rises and falls. But he cannot do anything, there is nothing more to be done. So he gets up and goes to the window. There is no one out on the street. It is a windless night, and the moonlight bathes the walls, making them look as though they have been freshly plastered.

Every now and then there is a noise – filtered, muffled. A sort of quiet buzzing. From far off, from who knows where, it rises like an echo, enveloping and containing all sounds.

He will not get back to sleep, he knows this too. And before long, in the silence of dawn, more tense than the silence of night, he might just want to think about her.

In fact he does, he thinks of her and of Nunzio, before the alarm rings, with all the unease that memories and tiredness leave in us. Once again, last summer in Acireale. Sitting close to each other on the terrace of the restaurant, looking at the sea. Out over the azure water, under the sun, the boats bob gently and just a bit farther out a motorboat produces some foam in its wake.

'I really have to tell you...'

He was looking at a rock at the entrance to the small harbour, almost as though it were a new thing; and then the dog-leg jetty in the midst of the houses and the steps down to the moorings, with two or three boats tied up there. And he would have liked other things to look at, to focus his mind on. So as not to look at her, and her strange smile. He had to in the end though, when she put her hand on his. And he had to listen to her, when she said it was the right thing for both of them. And he heard that his own voice was different when he asked:

'Why, Tina?'

'Because I can't do it. I can't go with you.' And after a moment, 'And have you really thought about it? You're an only child too. And my parents are older, they wouldn't understand...'

'Or is it you who doesn't understand?' he blurted out. 'Because you'd have to change town... your habits, your friends? And all of this just to marry a policeman?'

'That's not it, no... even you know you're being unfair now.'

'Explain it to me then.'

'It's pointless. And do you know why? It's because you don't want to understand. You have your own logic, your ideas. And when you've made up your mind, you have no consideration for others, you just stop thinking about them.'

In the harbour below the terrace the boats moved gently, tugged by a slight undertow. Things were different now... inside.

'Giovanni,' for a moment she was serious, then her face softened. 'I'm really sorry, but I've thought about it and I had to tell you. It's for the best...'

With the quiet splashing of the waves against the jetty, with the breath held and then let go again, it was as though time had stopped. Then he had picked up his glass and noticed that his hands were trembling. Ever since he had been promoted and came back to Catania less often, he was afraid of losing Tina, and this was absurd, because really he had never had her. He had not entered her mind, her blood – he was little more than a friend. Someone that could be relinquished. She had just told him that.

'It's right that you should live your life, that you should be free. You've studied hard, you want this... it's right,' she says now.

'What's right?'

'I understand, that's what I mean. You didn't have to...' she stops, now, breathing slowly. 'Didn't have to ask me for my opinion when you took the job...'

'So you don't want to come any more?'

'That's not it...'

'What is it then?'

'It's difficult to say. But this means being disloyal too.' Her voice cracks, for a moment. 'Your indifference to my projects, the lack of sharing... Sometimes I felt as though everything was just as it used to be, but now I feel that we've changed. Or rather, that only I'm the only one who hasn't changed...'

Cataldo has a sense of unease. A sense of pathetic embarrassment. 'We chose to live separately. And I haven't forgotten that.'

'That was how it should've been. But you can't, when there's nothing left. When you don't speak, don't listen. You don't feel the same things anymore.'

She has raised her voice to emphasize the words, as though making it easier to understand. He swallows, then decides. He has to ask her now, the question he has in his throat: 'Be honest. Is there someone else?'

Suddenly she frowns, and for a moment she looks almost ugly.

'How can you think that?'

'I'm thinking about Barone, surprise surprise... that lawyer Barone. He is a lawyer, isn't he?'

'You have no respect for me...'

'You were seen together. Walking in the Bellini Gardens.'

'So what?' But she denies everything, red in the face. 'No... no, there's no one. Not him, no one else. I swear...'

'Forget it, I'm serious now. I've known Barone for a long time. He's an egotist, he's in love with himself.'

She looks at him without seeing him: 'It's best if we change the subject. That's the best thing.'

'He'll give you a bad time. And I don't want that to happen.'

The indignation in her voice now carries irony in it: 'You think you know him because you did your military service together. But that was twenty years ago. People change over time. You've changed. That's exactly what we were saying... so why can't he have changed?'

'Because he can't have. I know him too well.'

'This is just jealousy talking.'

'True.' His fiery blushing does not stop him. 'I'm jealous of anyone who looks at you, but that doesn't stop me judging them accurately.'

She does not reply immediately. In the warm air a wasp buzzes, astonished by the silence it finds.

'Please think about it,' he said to her in the end, under his breath. 'Think about what we'd dreamed of doing.' There was a strange tranquillity in him, almost hope. Or was it resignation?

'I don't know. It's not the right choice.' And after a moment: 'There's nothing I can do.'

He was already expecting her to ask him to take her home.

She did not say a word all the way.

He has changed out of his pyjamas and now he is wandering around the house, not knowing what to do. In the end he looks at his watch and decides. Ten to seven, he knows her well, she is certainly up and dressed already. He lifts the receiver and dials the number:

'Hello, *Mamma*. How are you?'

'Giovanni!' And he can see her, mouth open in surprise.

'How are you?' he has to repeat.

'Me? Fine.'

'Really?'

'Yes, I told you. What about you... ?'

'You weren't asleep, were you?'

'No, no, not at all... you did the right thing phoning now. It costs less...'

'Well, how's it going?'

'Well, I can't complain. My legs are better and the heat's not too bad. Yesterday I even managed to go to the cemetery without taking the bus...'

'To see *Papà*, of course. Every Thursday.'

'I changed the water and left some fresh flowers. Then I came back home with Matilde... you remember her, don't you. We talked about you.'

'Thanks, *Mamma*' And he has a vision of his old nurse – moving slowly, slightly asthmatic, mending other people's clothes with determination and dedication. 'But tell me about you. How's work going?'

'Good. It's going. No time to get bored.' His voice becomes brighter as he puts on a mysterious air.

'I'm investigating two deaths up here. Important stuff...'

'Well... be careful, watch your step... sorry for telling you that. I know you're a grown man, but...'

'But you can never be too careful. I know, you're always telling me.' And after a pause: 'But don't you worry about me... in fact, when it's all over, I hope to come down... I can only manage five or six days, but it'd do me good.'

'That would be lovely, yes...' But she coughs, suddenly, and he knows it is not her throat. 'There's someone here who hasn't forgotten you...'

'Really, *Mamma*?'

'Yes, that's what I said.'

'Someone in particular?'

She does not reply, just breathes into the receiver.

'Chin up, *Mamma*. Keeping your chin up helps you feel better.'

'Right, well, this is what I wanted to tell you.' She hesitates before continuing: 'I saw Tina, yesterday.'

'Ah... where?'

'In town, in Piazza Dante. In front of the church, San Nicolò.'

'I see. And who was she with?'

'On her own, she was. Why? Who should she have been with?'

'I don't know. I was just asking... and did you talk?'

'Of course, two or three minutes. She was kind...'

'And what did she have to say?'

'Nothing about you, if you must know. But she wanted to... she wanted to say hello to you.'

'And how do you know that?'

'Because I wasn't born yesterday. I could tell. From her voice, from her face... it was shyness.'

'Tina? Shy?'

'Reserved, then... or embarrassed... that's what I think. You could see...'

'I understand... forget it. If I come back, I'll ask her myself...'

A waste of time, no point persisting with her and her badly hidden enthusiasm. She had grown truly fond of Tina, really wanted them married, but age does not always bring wisdom and Tina was not the right one for him and his *Mamma* could not see that. No fault of hers mind you. Even he had believed in it, only now did he see the truth. She was beautiful enough and had some good qualities – kind, tender, cheerful. But she would not have been a good wife. So why did he continue to think about her? That song was right – you realize it is all over when you fall into the suffering...

'Are you eating well?'

'Sorry, *Mamma*?'

'Up there I mean... are you eating well?'

'Ah... yes, fine. Sometimes I have supper in the trattoria.'

'On your own?'

'On my own, or with Muliere... I told you about him, didn't I?'

'Yes.'

'Every now and then, though. Because often I eat at home.'

'And you cook?'

'Me, yes. Why?' and he smiles. 'I manage, you know? Some spaghetti, some tinned meat, a piece of fruit...'

'Is that what you had yesterday?'

'Yesterday?' and his voice changes as Nunzio comes to his mind. 'No, not yesterday. I had some sandwiches.' He cannot tell her about the man who had his head smashed in.

'Come down as soon as you can, then. I'll make you a *caponata*, fish carpaccio and those almond biscuits you really like...'

'And no *cassata*?'

'We'll buy that from Giuffrida,' and she laughs.

'Alright then. As soon as I've finished this job.'

He hangs up with the sound of her laughter still in his ears. And he smiles too, but not for long. He has not told her everything about himself, which is normal. His life with its unsatisfied desires, a few murders and a lot of homesickness. No, he has not told her everything. He is well aware of that. Living is difficult, but it is even more difficult to explain it... life.

CHAPTER FIFTEEN

It always returns

The house is in the very centre of town, at the crossroads of two lanes so narrow that it is difficult to see the sky when you look up. Cataldo rings the bell at eight o'clock in the morning. Normally he would worry about disturbing people at this time, but not now, not after everything that has happened. As he waits for the intercom to croak into life he feels the heat that is already rising – the summer exploding from the earth, indifferent to the fear, the anxiety of men. Nearby a cat yawns, lying in a slice of sunlight, the only one on the pavement. He hears the dry click of the door being opened, without even a 'Who's there?' The entrance is cold and the stairs are damp, with a vague smell of mould. He reaches the second floor and Ramondini is already there with the door open: his eyes are puffy, almost as though he has not slept. But he does not seem particularly surprised when he focuses his gaze on Cataldo and shakes his hand. Indeed, he says: 'I knew it.'

'What?'

'That you'd come to see me. Not necessarily so soon... but I was expecting it, sooner or later...'

'Why?'

'It was my celebration, wasn't it? It was a special day for me, not for the others. The others were only guests...'

Cataldo says nothing, because he already understands.

'So I can guess what you want from me: is there anything I remember... did I make all the invitations and why. Did I keep photos as souvenirs...'

'Quite. Did you keep any?'

'It's only natural, isn't it?'

'Of course it is.' Cataldo starts, almost in anger. 'But why didn't you tell me immediately?'

'I don't know.' He spreads his arms, as though astonished. 'Perhaps because you didn't ask me...'

'What do you mean! That may well be true, but you all knew... you certainly all knew... that I was looking for those pictures. Any picture at all of that evening... but let's just forget it,' and he calms down, almost immediately. 'Just let me see them.'

'Of course,' says Ramondini. 'I'll go get them.' But he hesitates, standing there looking at Cataldo. 'If you really think it's worthwhile...'

'Yes, I think it is. And I'm not the only one.' The other man stares at him, his mouth open. And Cataldo adds: 'There's been another death. Last night. And the motive was one of those photos.'

The natural thing for Ramondini to do would be to ask who had been killed. But he does not ask. He simply nods, to say that he understands, and he goes. I wonder if he knew already, thinks Cataldo, standing there on his own. Or perhaps he hesitated just to avoid displaying a curiosity that could be taken wrongly, suspiciously. Ramondini returns after two or three minutes with an old-fashioned photo album, spiral bound, a floral pattern on its cover. He opens it at the first page, then steps backwards and remains there standing. Cataldo sits without being invited to do so. 'Sit down too,' he says to Ramondini and he starts leafing through.

The photos are clear, more so than he would have imagined. In one there are Miriam and Giulio Zoboli, the latter with his hand on her shoulder and holding a lit cigarette; alongside are Ramondini and Don Lodi, smiling towards the camera. In front of them is a white tablecloth, some plates, two or three bottles that look like spumante. In another photo Katia stands, not next to Zanetti, but next to Calabrese who is sitting, his hands on the tablecloth, both of them with a strange smile that seems a bit silly. Then there is a group photo of all seven together against a white wall under a clock that gives the time as ten o'clock – a classic souvenir photo taken during the evening. All posing, all smiling with the red-eye effect of the flash...

'What do you think?'

'That you've all come out very well.'

'No, seriously...'

'Well, you're all different. Much younger.'

'Right.' He does not pursue the point, just smiles in an almost melancholy way. 'You're right. When it's not death that changes people, it's life.'

And those words ring in his mind as he looks down once more to study the pictures. More of the same. The priest toasts Ramondini, face to face, perhaps the last toast of the evening because there is a waiter there to one side, against the same white wall, and he is busy clearing the table. Then the priest again, arm in arm with Ramondini and Zoboli, their heads bowed as though talking intently. That is all there is. There is no point going on because the photos that follow have nothing to do with that evening.

'That's it,' says Ramondini, and he opens his arms.

'Don't worry. It's not your fault...'

And Ramondini says nothing now. It is almost as though he struggles to make conversation, with all his culture and his university job. In the end, after thinking for a while, he asks, 'Do you want to keep them?'

'The photos? No thanks. I've seen all I need to. To be more precise, there's nothing there to see.'

And he explains to Ramondini who has not understood: 'Sometimes that's what happens. An object enters in some way into your life and it won't go away. For me at this moment it's a photograph.' He looks for something in his pocket, who knows what, and then gives up. 'I wonder which photo the killer took after killing Nunzio? It must be important since he risked so much.'

'Nunzio's dead?'

Cataldo stares at him, wondering for a moment if he is being honest. Then he nods: 'Just a few hours ago.'

'And... how?'

'Someone smashed his head in with a paperweight. Then this someone ripped a photo out of an old issue of *Guiglia Oggi*. Incredible, isn't it? But that's what happened. That was the motive. A photo that I wasn't supposed to see.'

He is on his feet now, walking around the room.

'Are you sure?'

He stops suddenly. 'Yes, I'm sure. Nunzio had an appointment with me, to show me that issue of the paper. An article perhaps with photos, like these...' And his jaw tightens with anger. 'And now I know there was a photo. Otherwise Nunzio wouldn't have been killed. But what type of photo? Like that one of you and Zoboli, for example? What does it all mean?'

He stops to catch his breath and the suddenly turns to look at Ramondini. For the first time the professor seems ill at ease.

'Zoboli. I heard you were friends, despite the age difference.'

'Just three years. That's not...'

'No, what I mean is that three years in themselves aren't much, but from other points of view they can be important. Zoboli just entering high school, you leaving high school. Zoboli a student at the university while you already had your degree...'

'I don't understand.'

'Zoboli with temporary jobs, you with tenure. It's important. You've always been – how shall I put it? – a point of reference for him. Someone more authoritative... I'm not even sure how to explain. And yet, despite this, you owed him something too... at least according to certain rumours I've heard.' He studies him now, waiting for a gesture, a reaction, or a change of expression. 'This is why I'm truly curious about the relationship you had... really... above and beyond what the others think, even above and beyond this investigation.'

'What do you mean, above and beyond the investigation?'

'I mean I really don't know, believe me... whether your relationship in some way influenced his death. Perhaps not, not in the slightest. But I'd like to know. I'd like to understand you both better. That's why I'm asking you, and please don't be offended, whether Zoboli made – how shall I put it? – made some contribution to your career...'

'A contribution?'

'Yes. To your publications, or in some other way.' He tries, as much as possible, to weigh his words. 'Whether you might have used, even if the evidence says the opposite...'

'Whether I might have exploited him, you mean?'

'Well, yes... let's try putting it that way.'

Ramondini seems smilingly indifferent. 'I think you're making a mistake, if you believe what Zoboli's wife says—

in love with her husband to the point where she can't see the truth. Even though he didn't deserve it...'

'No?'

'No... but I don't want to say anything else, it's not my business, especially now that he's dead. What I do want to say is that I've never copied anything from him, or exploited his work in any way whatsoever. We worked together, that's true... but in the sense that I gave him research to do and he did it – with me directing him of course – and in the end we compared notes and I made the final corrections...'

Cataldo wants to ask whose name went on the publications. But it is best for now to let him finish.

'So... as you can see, it's something quite different. This isn't exploitation...'

It might even be true, if it were not for his insistent denials, a slight anxiety that betrays the conscious desire to be believed.

'... and all this despite anything Miriam may have said.'

Cataldo smiles: 'Actually Miriam doesn't come into this at all, it was my idea. Ever since Don Lodi told me that you two were different, but complementary. You are hard-working, consistent, while Zoboli was – how did he put it? – yes... intuitive, acute. Although he was more sporadic and less confident. So I reckoned...'

'Your reckoning's wrong, believe me.'

'Alright, let's drop it. And Don Lodi?'

'Sorry?'

'I mean... what's the relationship there? He says he values you very much, that he was right about you from your schooldays... and he's very gratified by this fact, it seems. He certainly values your intellect...'

'So?'

'So I don't understand the human side of it... your relationship. You... excuse me, but you're not married...'

'Is that so strange?'

'Certainly not.' And Cataldo smiles again behind the tension. 'You're not married, I was saying, and you've never gone out with anyone. Don Lodi seems to admire you for this... for the fact that you've never been distracted...'

'And perhaps you find it strange... they'll have told you about this I imagine. You find it strange that we've been on holiday together?'

'No, I didn't know that. The two of you?'

'It was a study holiday! Frankfurt, for a conference! Didn't they mention that? Does that seem strange too?'

He is over excited now and realizes it immediately. So he starts explaining: 'I'm sorry, but the fact is that we've always been in love... no, don't misunderstand me. We've always been in love with the same things, the same studies – literature, philosophy. We've studied, discussed, compared notes together regularly. Faithfully over the years. The same things. Without some sort of long-term trial, nothing, nothing at all can keep people united...'

He holds his hands on his knees as he speaks, and his fingers continue to contract and open, almost as though he cannot decide whether to clench them into fists or not.

Cataldo nods and says, 'Fidelity, of course. Fidelity is very important in studies, as you said. But it's also important in friendship. And in love... a thought has come to me, as you were speaking...'

And he says nothing now. In fact he turns and coughs, takes a handkerchief and blows his nose. But Cataldo sees a red blotch appear on his neck and watches it flush upwards, right up to his ears.

*

She is there in front of him at ten o'clock in the morning. They are in a cool, shady room in her villa. The biggest villa of them all, one of the new ones near the swimming pool. She was easy to find and he studies her now as he thanks her for her kindness, and he cannot get the idea out of his mind that she must have been a beautiful woman. Tall, about seventy, her grey hair neat, a gold chain round her neck, a moss-green gaberdine dress. She looks so cool that it is as though she does not feel the heat, or as though she has not been out of the house yet that morning. Only later does he notice the curtain that hangs from the ceiling, keeping the room in shade and muffling the sounds of the life that goes on outside. Because where they are now, in the dated atmosphere of that room, it is as though time has stood still. On the furniture, on a table, everywhere there are photographs, especially of children, most in slightly tatty leather frames. But there is a silver one too, tarnished with time, and in it the photograph of a girl in a wedding gown and on each side of it another photograph – one a carabiniere, the other a naked baby on a cushion. And as he looks around he follows her to the end of the room, towards a sofa and two armchairs, and he sits in the one she points to. She takes her place on the sofa, calmly, and she puts a cushion behind her back. Arthritis may have slowed down her movements, but her mind is still acute and rapid, Cataldo sees this immediately.

'Why?'

He does not reply but stares, motionless, out of the window that looks out over the road. A shutter perhaps moves, but it cannot have been the wind.

'Why?' she repeats, and perhaps now there is a slight tone

of irritation in her voice. 'Why dig up the past? Everything was said and written eighteen years ago. You know that fine well.'

'In the newspapers, yes. And at the trial. I've read the documents.' Cataldo leans forward, speaks in a deep voice. 'But in my work I've also come to understand something.'

'Which is?'

'Which is that you can never do the truth justice in an official summary. Because the things that count are the ones that are left out – the emotions, the feelings. People's characters. These are all things that can't appear in a document.'

He looks at her intently, but he is not hoping that she will confide in him. And yet she does starts speaking, a little tiredness in her voice.

'Eighteen years have gone by, but I still remember everything. When he died and even before that, long before that. The marriage, our life together. But it's only natural in the end. When we're old we have more memories than we have hopes.'

'Tell me about it, if you want to.'

She sighs. 'I met him when I was just a girl. At a schoolfriend's party. You know... the type of party that teenagers used to have – records, cakes and parents on the other side of the door.'

'Things were different, it's true,' he says, smiling.

'I fell in love immediately, like the girl I was. He was my first love,' she says quietly, as though justifying herself. 'After university, we got married...'

'Did Don Lodi officiate?'

Cataldo's question appeared spontaneously, with no precise motive. She shakes her head and her face takes on a strange expression.

'I don't know why I asked that... but you do know him, don't you?'

'Everyone here knows him.'

'And you?'

'Me?'

'What do you think of him?'

'Don Athos? Well... I don't know...' and she thinks, looking ill at ease. 'A modern priest, I suppose,' she says in the end. But it is obvious that it took some effort to come up with this.

'You were telling me that you got married...'

'Yes. But Marco was born later, when I'd already started teaching...'

'So I've been told. History, I think...'

'At the scientific high school.'

And since she stops speaking, to make sure the conversation does not die out, he says, 'I have a lot of respect, you know, for your profession.'

'Are you just saying that out of courtesy?'

'I say that because I mean it. My mother was a teacher too, and I have good memories of my own teachers. Almost all of them, really. Honest people. A bit ingenuous, but uncompromising...' He smiles with a conviction that comes from the phrase that has come to his mind. 'There was a writer who once said, rightly, that whoever teaches is like a trainer... but not of bodies, of brains, which are a lot trickier.'

Now she smiles too. For the first time.

'He was right. Indeed, teaching has been the best experience life has given me.'

'More than your marriage?'

'More than anything else, yes.' She says it quickly and Cataldo looks at her, but she does not regret having said it.

She just sighs and concentrates, like someone about to confess.

'I don't think I would have remained married to him till the very end, if it hadn't been for... yes, if he hadn't died.'

Cataldo wants to ask why, but he stops himself. Perhaps she will tell him anyway.

'Because you can forgive many things. It's normal when desire dies... one or two affairs. But an arid heart is unforgivable.' She closes her eyes, just for a moment.

'Especially when faced with pain...'

'When did you hear that he'd died?'

'My cousin came here to the house. He was crying, he couldn't even speak. Then he scribbled on a sheet of paper, 'Walter's dead'. I sat down to watch the television, who knows what programme it was, and I didn't cry.' Then a pause before she adds, 'I cried later.'

She shakes her head and for a moment it is almost as though she does not want to continue. 'Why am I telling you all this? I haven't spoken about it for years...'

'But you've thought about it. You've always been thinking about it.'

'Yes,' and she nods two or three times.

'But it's good to talk, sometimes. Whatever the reason was for the silence – reserve, shyness... even remorse...'

'Perhaps you're right,' and she looks at him. 'It's guilt that lies behind some silences.'

'Why don't you carry on then?' And since she says nothing, he adds, 'Speaking, I mean. Because there's something I've been wanting to ask you for some time now. Why on earth did your husband have all that money with him that night?'

And in her eyes there is a flash of fear before she manages

to appear serious, alert.

'You know why, Inspector. Everyone knows. He was buying a villa... nearby, in Gainazzo. Ever been there?'

'No,' he admits, indifferent.

'A nineteenth-century villa, with stables, built on the Montecuccoli rock. A bargain. My cousin from Tecnodomus handled the deal... the owner was up to his eyes in debt or had to move, I can't remember... so there was this opportunity to snap it up for such a low price... only he wanted cash and as soon as possible...'

'Yes,' Cataldo agrees. 'That's what you said at the trial. Exactly that.'

'And what do you think?'

He shakes his head. 'It doesn't matter what I think. What matters is what I know.'

She swallows, lowers her eyes. And when she looks up into Cataldo's eyes the question – what do you know? – is so obvious she does not have to utter it.

'I know, for a start, that it's just not believable that someone goes to buy real estate at night with seven hundred million lire in cash, like a thief. Not even for the purpose of tax evasion... a bank transfer would make much more sense. And then there's the legal side... contracts, solicitors, all that. No, no... even you must see that it doesn't add up...'

'But everyone believed me at the trial.'

'Because the aim of that investigation and trial was different. They were looking for the person who stole that money, not for an explanation as to why the money was there at midnight, in a suitcase...' He continues to stare at her. 'That's what I'm interested in. Now.'

'There's nothing I can do if you think it's unbelievable. But that's how things went...'

153

But there is a slight crack in her obstinacy, a trace of fatigue. He sighs, patiently: 'Come on, Signora. Don't you think after so many years it's time to tell the truth? Two people have died for that money. The latest died last night. Have you heard?'

'No... I don't read the newspapers... who was it?'

The tone of her voice is slightly higher now, almost as though she were trying to create a screen for her agitation.

'Nunzio Napolitano.'

'From the tourist office?'

'That's him.'

'I'm sorry.'

'Did you know him?'

She nods. For a moment it looks as though she is going to cry, but she does not. Her voice is expressionless now: 'I don't know what to say.'

'I can help you, if you like. With an idea. Just tell me if I'm wrong or if I'm right.' He stands up, turns his eyes to the ceiling. 'When I read about all that money I thought of two things... the only possible things. First, blackmail... perhaps something to do with work. But up here extortion and bribes are rare, and your husband wasn't a businessman on the national scene... and then that amount of money was too much... for 1980 at least. So then I thought of the other thing...'

He stops now and looks at her. The room is silent, but outside, somewhere, a car alarm has gone off.

'Kidnapping. That's what I thought of. And at this point everything became clear in just one possible way. Who was the person closest to you... the only person you would have paid such a ransom for?'

She is petrified now. Almost as though she has stopped

breathing. She looks into space beyond Cataldo. But still she does not cry.

'Is that what it was, then?'

'It always returns,' she whispers. 'The remorse, the anguish. It never goes away.'

'It's the past that never goes away. Sometimes a whole life isn't enough.'

There is something dignified in her stillness, like an ancient statue. And in her defeat. Because there is another torment, the biggest one.

'Perhaps there's something else?'

She looks at him, her eyes red: 'After eighteen years?'

'Yes.' And a book he once read comes to his aid, suddenly: 'Because we owe respect to the dead, while to the living we owe the truth.'

She surrenders now: 'You tell me. It's easier for me if you say it.'

'There's just one thing to say.' He sits down again. 'There never was any kidnapping.'

'Yes.'

'Marco, your son, did it all. Perhaps he hated you both, perhaps just his father. Perhaps he needed money... or all these things together, I don't know. The fact is he organized everything. He pretended he had been kidnapped and demanded the ransom.'

Cataldo's throat is dry now, but he has almost finished.

'I understood it all from the newspapers. He was the only one missing at the funeral. And he was an only child. So I wondered, ever heard of an only child that fails to go to his father's funeral? Unless he was ill or abroad or doing some important job somewhere. It would have to be some incredibly important commitment or reason... like a kidnapping, for example. He couldn't turn up straight away, after having led everyone on about the kidnapping. And you really had to be convinced, didn't you?'

She strokes her cheek, gets her breath back.

'But then he reappeared, a week later more or less, to help with the investigation. That's what the papers said. And for me the obvious question was why did they free the hostage if they never received the money? And then I understood.'

He does not tell her that in her son's favour, he had thought that the kidnappers had dazzled her husband's car before taking the money. But he had excluded this hypothesis almost immediately. Indeed, professional kidnappers would have waited without interfering, hidden away somewhere, for the money to be delivered...

'He wasn't a bad boy.' Her voice is increasingly tired, lower. 'He studied, he was kind... it was the drugs that ruined him.'

'How did you find out?'

'About the kidnapping? He told me, before he died. He was conscious. He asked my forgiveness, and I forgave him. He'd be your age now, more or less...'

Cataldo could be her son, yes. He had thought about that. The son she would like to have had.

'I promised I'd never tell anyone and today I've betrayed him. Perhaps it's because I wanted to talk about it, to share the weight... or perhaps it's because you remind me of him. I don't see many young people, at my age...'

Cataldo perceives some pent-up emotion in her voice, a raw tenderness. And now he wants to promise something. 'As far as I'm concerned, you can rely on me not to tell anyone anything. I give you my word. Don't worry.'

He stands up and she smiles at him, sadly.

'Don't worry? Peace of mind's a thing I no longer know. I've lost all that in the course of my life...'

He does not know what to say, so all he can offer is, 'Again, I'm sorry.'

He shakes her hand in the entrance. A ray of sun enters from the half-open door.

'I'll come back to visit, if I may.'

She looks at him in a strange way, as if such things were no longer important. As if she were struggling under the weight of a sudden tiredness.

'The elderly are like the seats in a theatre – all the gilt-work faded, peeling... old existences in need of replacement. So much has passed before our eyes...'

Cataldo judges it to be a fine phrase, appropriate from a well-read teacher. But he knows that she means every one of those words. And so he takes his leave feeling very sad indeed.

CHAPTER SIXTEEN

A third dead man

Standing there, sweating in the sun. There is no one around now. The thought comes that everyone is at home, or in the hotel, sitting down to lunch. Then a siesta, a little nap. From somewhere comes the voice of a television newsreader. You can tell by the timbre – strong, regular. And the neutral accent.

To go in now, or to wait? The clock says a quarter past one – that is alright. But it is difficult to make a decision. And the sweat continues to pour, but it's not because of the heat. Suddenly a noise from behind, like a rapping on the pavement, but there is no one there – it's just nerves. And now, there before the glass doors, the reflection is of a different face – pale and ugly. For a moment it is unrecognizable.

A decision is made. Out of the left-hand pocket the shadow pulls an envelope, holds it between its teeth, while from the same pocket it extracts a pair of thin rubber gloves. Gloves or anything that interferes with the sense of touch have always been anathema, but they will be necessary for this job. The envelope is placed back in the pocket, the fingers inserted one by one and then the sleeves of the gloves rolled out above the wrists. The Beretta 7.65 weighs a bit in the other pocket, on the right-hand side. Instinctively, one hand goes to touch the pistol through the fabric and arranges it so that the handle is lying upwards.

The word CLOSED is written on the sign, but there is no doubt that the door is unlocked – a deep breath and the shadow pushes it open. Blood hammers in the temples, the heart rises – once again – to the mouth. The pulse beats in the chest, in the neck, in the wrists. The door opens and closes slowly – not a sound, not a squeak. Inside all is silent, just the noise of that beating heart and the breathing.

There is no one in the first room, just furniture and papers. The computer is switched off, the desk is empty, the brochures are on the table. Then there is that panel, with its coloured notices. The first one, at the top, advertises a house out in the country, at Roccamalatina.

'Oh, it's you. I was expecting you.'

The voice comes as a surprise, from the right, three or four metres away, down the corridor. Evidently he was in one of the rooms and heard some noise. So a hand goes to the pocket, pulls out the envelope and puts it on the desk. Their eyes meet and Zanetti smiles as he approaches. Perhaps he has not noticed the gloves, or has not given them a second thought.

It is the barrel of the pistol that stops him. It transforms his smile into a start of surprise. But he still does not understand. He seems surprised, not frightened. His chest, under the t-shirt, rises and falls with the rhythm of his breath. He stares at the Beretta with some uncertainty.

'You're joking?'

'No.'

And now he understands that he is to die. His stomach contracts, drops of sweat appear at his temples, in his armpits. He stands rigid, holding his breath now, almost as though this might be enough to make him invisible. But it is too late.

'*Addio*, Carlo.'

A feeling of impotence, of controlled, profound desperation. And the fear now. Fear that grips his guts, dries his mouth, leaving in it the taste of copper. Because he had never thought of dying like this. He has lost control of the game now, a game in which he was outclassed by his opponent...

The bullet hits him in the chest, driving him against the wall. A flower of blood appears on the white t-shirt. The lancing pain shoots through his belly and paralyzes him. Suddenly his mouth is full of blood. He gargles, suffocating, still standing. Then he leaves the wall and goes to take a step, swaying – before the darkness in his eyes, the unconsciousness, darkens his mind forever.

The killer picks the envelope up again, puts it back in the pocket it came from. Then the killer moves towards the victim, arm extended. One more shot in the chest before leaving, without looking back. Carlo falls backwards, kicks violently at nothing and lies there, motionless. The only thing hanging in the air is the smell of gunpowder.

CHAPTER SEVENTEEN

Behind the scenes

It is six in the evening and they have all left. Cataldo is alone in the Tecnodomus offices. To the naked eye, very little evidence remains of what has happened – just some blood and the chalked contours of the body's position. And in his mind the image of the holes in Zanetti's chest, one just above his heart, before they took him away with the brisk professionalism they always display. And his friend's face, the one who had found him just after three o'clock, pushing open the door that had been left ajar – his noisy grief and his swearing which for some reason had not shocked Cataldo. At that moment, in that way, it did not seem disrespectful.

And now he thinks, he has always thought, that there is always a behind-the-scenes, even for these crimes. And what happens after, behind the scenes, is that when they have taken the bodies away and the detectives leave too, together with the forensics team, then there is nothing left at the crime scene, apart from the blood stains and the disorder left first by the killer, then by investigators like him and then all that is left is the grief of the survivors. Like Katia, Zanetti's wife, who is waiting in the car in front of the office, Muliere by her side. Cataldo has asked her to wait.

He walks through the first room, then along the corridor. He opens and closes the doors of the other two rooms and looks at everything without seeing anything. His mind is busy with the few certainties he has. Zanetti knew his killer and the weapon must be the same one that was used to kill Zoboli – he feels these things. And this death is connected with the others: Zoboli Nunzio Zanetti, a cruel chain, but not an absurd one. There must be a logic, a motive, even though he still has not brought it into focus and something is missing. A link, an idea...

He sighs now, shakes his head. Best get going, he is just wasting time here. He walks out, locks the door and puts the key in his pocket. Then he opens the car door on the driver's side. Muliere nods, gets out to give him his seat and leaves, without saying a word.

They are silent for a few seconds, delicate and tense seconds, before the questions. He has to choose where to start. He could ask her for an alibi for the early afternoon – it has to be done anyway and that would buy him some time, and in any case she does not seem to be too upset. A lack of emotion, that is what she displays. There are some signs of grief on her face, but it is as though something is being held back, repressed, by a veil of disbelief. But then he knows just how easy it is to misinterpret the disorientation caused by grief. And just how inadequate the initial reaction to a trauma can appear to be. So he decides not to ask about the alibi for now. He concentrates, looks her in the eye. He chooses a phrase of condolence, one of the conventional ones, but she interrupts him, without being impolite.

'Please. I appreciate your courtesy, but it's not necessary.' And then after a moment, 'I have to tell you some things that I'd prefer you learnt directly from me.'

'For example?'

'For example, my... how can I put it... well, yes, my lack of grief.'

'If you want to describe it that way...' he says, carefully.

'It's not that I want to. I have to.'

'Why?'

She makes a gesture with her hand – impotence or resignation. 'Because it was all over, had been for some time. Even though we continued to live together, and perhaps people didn't know...'

'Why?' he asks again, slightly uneasy.

'There is no reason behind some things. Falling in love at twenty is easy for anyone. The difficult thing is staying in love. That's what happened to us.'

'If you agree to live together, then together you save yourselves or you lose yourselves,' says Cataldo suddenly. He sounds like a priest, but it does not matter because he believes it and he realizes this as soon as the words come out. She looks at him, perhaps surprised.

'What does that mean?'

'It means that life is made up of boring moments as well. Or of difficult moments. The important thing is to live through them together.'

It is the second time he has used that word. This time she approves.

'You're right. Together – that's love.' She thinks for a moment and then adds, 'To love someone you have to believe in the same idea of life. You have to want the same things.'

'And he no longer wanted them?'

'No. He changed first. Then I changed, too, after he did...'

'After him... did you hate him for that?'

She shakes her head, passionless. 'We choose people. And it's our own fault if they make us suffer, or if they make us become worse people...'

There is something missing here, but he does not pursue it. Instead he asks, 'Why didn't you separate?'

'Because of Luca. Our son.'

He nods as he remembers and asks another question, 'Was he in love with another woman?'

'Why do you ask me that?'

'Because no one worries about sex any more, but they do worry about feelings. Feelings frighten people.'

She reflects before answering, 'I never knew of anything.'

'And you?'

'Me?'

'Yes. Another man?'

A moment's hesitancy before she says, 'No. No one.'

A very common sort of story, in the end. At least according to what she has to say. The years go by, the passion ends where indifference begins. But there is something different. There is this violence, now, that has suddenly destroyed the resignation, the sadness. And there is a fair dose of nostalgia too.

'You realize, don't you, that your husband was killed by someone he knew well?' he asks suddenly.

'How do you know that?'

'Because he waited behind in the office, alone, with the closed sign on the door. Of course, he may have had urgent work to do and didn't want to be disturbed, I'd thought of that. But why did he leave the door open, or open it personally to someone outside of office hours? There's no sign of a break-in and the agency, with so few rooms, certainly isn't the type of place a killer could hide in before it closed...'

He stops here because an idea has come to him. 'Did your husband usually eat at home?'

'He usually did, yes.'

'And did he phone this time, to say he wouldn't be coming?'

'No.'

'You see? He must have had some important reason for changing his routine. A specific appointment, for example...'

She listens in silence, objects to nothing.

'That's why I wonder: who hated your husband so much?'

For the first time she seems worried. 'I don't know. No one I know of. Why are you asking me this?'

'Because hate might be a motive in this crime. Two shots fired at close range. The desire to kill... you understand?'

And the reply comes in a whisper, 'In hatred there's always a lot of love.'

And this time too there is something missing. To what or to whom do these words allude? But it does not matter. He has to bring their conversation back to more concrete topics.

'Your husband was a partner in Tecnodomus with Calabrese. Right?'

'Yes.'

'Tell me about that.'

'About the business?'

'That too. Did your husband have – how shall I put it? – enemies in this field? I don't know... particularly hostile competitors?'

'To the point where they'd kill him? I doubt it. But I've already told you I know nothing about this...'

'So let's move on to something you know more about. His relationship with Calabrese.'

She seems perturbed now. 'We're friends...'

'If you're friends, then you know about your husband's relationship with him.'

'They were partners.'

'I know. But were they good partners?'

She remains silent, does not commit.

'Did you hear what I asked?'

'No. They weren't good partners. And the worst was yet to come.'

'What do you mean?'

'Well... Carlo had bought Tecnodomus on his own in 1981. Don't ask me where he got the money, because I really don't know... then two years later, out of the blue, he asked Franco to come in as his partner...'

'With fresh capital... I see. But was there anything behind this move?'

'There was something. Some difficulty, a debt. And the extra money was useful.'

'How do you know this?'

'I was the bait. That's not the right word, but you understand. I approached Franco, rekindled the friendship... in the end I was the one who convinced him...'

'And now you're sorry you did that.'

'Yes.' And a pause before, 'And I'm sorry about another thing.'

'Tell me about it.'

'Let's call it ingratitude. After all I did for him, my husband was about to abandon Franco. Get out of it... you understand?'

'Not really.'

'Out of the business, at the drop of a hat, stabbing Franco in the back.' Her voice for a moment cracks, quavers in contempt. 'Over the years I'd come to know him to be superficial, frivolous, but never dishonest. And this was a really dirty trick.'

'Are you sure?'

'Yes, there's no doubt about it. I heard him, by chance,

talking with a lawyer who explained the legal situation to him.' She concentrates and then recites almost from memory, 'According to a Supreme Court decision of 1996 regarding private companies, if the partnership no longer exists due to a withdrawal then the remaining partner becomes accountable after six months for all the company's debts... It really was a move made with malice aforethought.'

'So Calabrese...'

'Yes, that's right. He would have been set up.'

'So there were debts?'

She nods. 'I don't know how much, but there were problems.'

Cataldo thinks for a moment about this last point, the most important. He is trying to make the connection with a motive.

'Have you told Calabrese?'

'Me? No... not yet.'

But she seems reticent, uneasy, perhaps even insincere. Or perhaps she is just a bit confused.

It is hot, in the car, but he does not think about switching on the air conditioning. He is very much engrossed in the flow of his thoughts. He well knows that the elements of truth in an enquiry often gradually acquire new meanings. To the point where sometimes they resemble a weave of signals, of clues pertaining to the possibility of different destinies, or they reveal fragments of some new reality. Because the crime is often the confirmation of a mystery that is already completely in the world, existing in things. But he also knows that the desire to find the truth leads the investigator to look for relationships between facts that are near and far in space and in time, to spot analogies, to pick up on coincidences, however strange or bizarre. All this as he descends the stairs of knowledge, along the darkest steps of the secret of being. Behind the apparent normality of human relations.

In this case, for example, if Marchisio was right, whoever stole those millions of lire in 1980 became rich from that moment on. It certainly could have been Zoboli: that detached villa did not match the salary of a temporary teacher. Zanetti too: a failed footballer who suddenly buys a real estate company one year later, perhaps he was driving that night. But both have been killed. And both of them with a pistol and by someone who knew them well. But this time there was a difference. Zanetti was about to screw his partner. Yes, this was different. He had at least to check up on Calabrese's alibi.

The car moves surely, almost as though it knows the way – the row of terraced homes, each with a low gate and a balcony. He stops in front of number 15 where he finds a space, just like last time. It's almost seven, Cataldo says to himself, he won't be eating. And instinctively he looks up at the window, the curtains closed as the last rays of sun make the glass shine. And he sees him this time too. His face again at the window, looking out, as though he had never moved. But this time it is not anger he sees on his face. Rather it is uncertainty... or fear.

When he reaches the door Calabrese has already taken the chain off and is ready to let him in. Inside everything is the same, but he seems different. Cataldo realizes this by the way he wheels the chair, more slowly now, almost as though it is a struggle for him. And then his face, which Cataldo can scrutinize well now as he sits opposite in an armchair. Neither of them speaks.

Calabrese seems overcome by a great tiredness, but he is trying to resist it. He has dark circles round his eyes and his skin is so pale that his lips, by contrast, seem to be painted on. And this silence – while there is nothing embarrassing or hostile in it – must be making him feel uneasy, because it facilitates the examination that Cataldo carries out and of which the other man is conscious; for this reason, even if it is an effort, Calabrese himself breaks it: 'So you've come back, Inspector. To keep me company? Or are you still not convinced about my condition?' But he coughs now, several times, and has to stop talking, his face red. And when he recovers he says, 'Can you imagine me on this chair, wheeling myself around Guiglia to shoot my friends?'

'I've never imagined that. And if I've given you that impression, let me apologise immediately.'

It is a truce of sorts, also because Cataldo smiles. And Calabrese smiles too, but rather than a smile his face seems to open up for a moment into a confused expression of bitterness, of irony for Cataldo and of tenderness, or indulgence for himself.

'So why have you come?'

'Is it such an intrusion?'

'No. I'm just curious.'

'I'm curious too. That's it... curiosity is the right word. I'm here out of curiosity.'

'And what interests you so much, about me?' He runs his hand across his forehead, a nervous gesture, for the third time. Perhaps the truce is already over.

'Your money. Or rather... let's say, when your wealth was born.'

'Well... when I made the money, you mean?'

'That's it.'

'And why?'

'Because... and don't be offended... whoever stole seven hundred million lire eighteen years ago from a Mercedes, the same night as Ramondini's party... whoever that was obviously became very rich...'

'Or must have multiplied his own money since then, if he already had money to start with. I appreciate frankness, Inspector. Your reckoning has brought you to me.' Perhaps he would like to joke about it, but irony does not come to his aid. 'Well... I'm sorry, but I'm afraid my wealth began to grow in the 1980s, more or less. Of course, I'd have to look in my files...'

How nice it would be, Cataldo thinks in the meantime, to be able to close his eyes against the white light that filters through the half-closed windows, while the curtains project their undulating shadows on the ceiling...

'I'm serious, you know.'

'I'm serious too! I may well have started saving money in the year that guy died, or was killed... who knows. And so? Is that a crime? It's true that I made money back then, but it was all invested very well in the stock market and even in bonds. I challenge anyone to show otherwise!'

'I hope you're able to prove all this...'

'Of course I can! And listen, I've had enough! I see no reason to continue a conversation that's threatening to go downhill.'

He is upset, he has raised his voice. Cataldo decides to calm things.

'Don't be offended, I said. After all, you have to admit that at least that I've been frank with you.'

'That's true.'

'So... remember we've just had a chat. A chat, you understand. I was just testing the waters.' He gets up calmly. 'I apologise for the visit. And don't worry, I know the way...'

He starts walking towards the entrance when Calabrese says, 'Inspector...'

Cataldo stops and smiles.

'Tell me at least whether you believe me or not.'

'Perhaps I do... but again, there's no need to show me out, please.' And then, when he is already out of sight he adds, 'Ah... I was forgetting. There was a letter for you hanging out of your box. I'll leave it here, near the telephone...'

From the other room comes Calabrese's thank you. Then the noise of the door closing. Then silence. A few seconds later comes the muffled squeak of the wheelchair. Then the sound of Calabrese lifting himself up out of the chair, standing and taking hold of the letter. His eyes are full of a satisfied, mischievous light.

CHAPTER EIGHTEEN

Coup de théâtre

'I really don't think it'll be of much interest to you.'

Cataldo's voice comes from behind and the mirror in the entrance transmits his smile as the light in Calabrese's eyes mutates into an expression of fear.

'It's my car insurance... it's about to expire. Been in my pocket since I picked it up this morning.' And he takes the letter delicately from Calabrese's hand and puts it away. 'Yup... I still haven't forked out for the premium...'

The invalid cannot speak – his throat is too tight. It is an absurd image, but now for Cataldo Calabrese looks like an automaton whose energy is completely exhausted. There is a sort of shame that paralyzes every reaction. Only after a minute or two, with an enormous effort, does he manage to say something.

'How... ?'

'The cleaning lady.'

'But I haven't got one.'

'Exactly.'

He makes a gesture inviting him to follow into the living room. Calabrese does so tamely, offering no resistance as he walks. And before he sits in an armchair, Cataldo takes a look at the wheelchair against one of the walls in the entrance. No need for that now.

'It was the cleaning lady that made me suspicious right from the first time I came. How could an invalid, a rich one at that, live alone without a woman, a nurse... someone? And this place is so tidy.'

He looks at Calabrese who has also taken a seat now and has started passing his hand across his forehead again.

'Everything spick and span... and that's how I guessed you were hiding something from me...'

He stops, offering the other man the chance to speak, but Calabrese continues staring at the floor between his shoes – silent. And Cataldo goes on: 'So I shut the door, but I didn't leave. Yup. You ought to be more careful – listen out for the footsteps as someone walks away.'

Silence, again. Cataldo looks around, feeling thirst building but there is nothing available to cure his dry throat. Pity.

'That's curiosity for you. But I'm not ashamed of it... curiosity isn't a defect. Quite the contrary, don't you think? When someone's left with no curiosity, he's stopped living.'

Impressions are strange things sometimes. Just a few minutes have gone by, but it seems to him that the glare has reduced and the half-light has increased. And this reminds him it is time to bring things to a conclusion.

'So... isn't it best if you tell me everything now?'

'Yes.'

He leans forward now, his elbows on his knees, his head in his hands. And when he starts speaking, it is almost a whisper. But for Cataldo this does not matter, it is enough that he talks and that he does not stop.

'I never did have polio. I let people believe that when I came to Modena... no one knew me anyway. The truth is different.'

'And?'

'I was knocked down in Switzerland when I was twelve. Very ordinary, isn't it? I was crossing the road at a zebra crossing... they certified me as a permanent invalid and the insurance company gave my parents an enormous sum in compensation. Then my mother died, my father had to move because of his job, but he'd invested the money well and now I have a guaranteed income. That's it.'

'That's not it. What about your status as an invalid?'

'Well you've seen what happened.'

'When?'

'Over time. After we came back to Italy.' Involuntarily he stretches his legs and lifts his elbows from his knees. 'I had a series of rehabilitation courses in a clinic I'd rather not name. Near Modena.'

'A lengthy business, I imagine.'

'Lengthy and difficult. Physiotherapy, hydrotherapy, orthopaedic devices... it took ages and a lot of determination. And all this without telling anyone.' He suddenly smiles. 'Can you believe that my classmates never suspected a thing? For two afternoons every week I simply wasn't there and twice a month I missed school in the morning, always on the same day of the week...'

'Until you got better.'

'Not really. The problem hasn't gone completely. It's just less serious.'

'Much less serious from what I've seen.'

'Yes.'

'But you continued to let everyone believe...'

'I know, I know...' He has lifted his eyes without moving his body and the line of his gaze is strangely oblique. 'I know I made a mistake... you can't imagine how often I have thought that. At home, alone, always... but I couldn't, you must understand that I couldn't.' He starts leaning forward again, his voice becomes a whisper, 'Once I'd started, I had to carry on.'

'Out of pride as well?'

'That too.'

'Because it was better, much better that everyone believed your wealth to have come from your intelligence. As an investor, an accountant... that's it, isn't it?'

'Yes.'

'So that you'd be noticed... perhaps even admired by people who might otherwise reject you. Physically, I mean...'

'Yes,' he repeats.

'Katia most of all?'

This time he does not reply.

'But lying is tiring and it leads to silence, to loneliness,' Cataldo says now, almost to himself. And Calabrese nods as Cataldo continues, 'And your appearance can never save you. It's just a screen. An illusion too.'

'But I haven't killed anyone... that's the truth! This is where my money came from... it wasn't stolen!' And he is almost shouting now as he repeats, 'I haven't killed anyone. I'm not capable of stealing, of killing. Not on principle but out of sheer cowardice.' And his last words are almost murmured. For a moment Cataldo feels he believes him, understands him. A sick meekness, indeed a sort of cowardice, born of the desire to avoid suffering, to hide himself; and over the years this had become passive contemplation of others, of their lives. Perhaps even envy on occasions. But not hatred, not a vendetta. Perhaps because those things require courage. But is all this the truth?

'So you didn't kill him?'

'No, no.'

'But who are we talking about?'

'About Zoboli.'

'Who mentioned Zoboli?' Cataldo studies him carefully. 'I'm not talking about Zoboli. I'm talking about Zanetti.'

Calabrese's eyes widen suddenly. As though Cataldo had uttered some magic word.

'Why Zanetti?'

'Because he was killed too, this afternoon. And you're not the cripple you claimed to be.'

Words that fall like stones in the silence. A silence that seems infinite and that Cataldo does nothing to break until the moment comes for the question, the question he has come here to ask.

'Where were you today, between one and three o'clock?'

He looks amazed, almost as he fails to understand, then he looks at the white wall behind Cataldo.

'Did you hear me?'

'Yes.'

'And you have to think about the answer?'

'No... I'm sorry. I was here... right here, reading.'

'Alone, I imagine.'

'Yes.'

'That's a shame though.'

'Why?'

'Because an alibi would have been useful for you.'

'An alibi?'

'Of course. Someone who'd seen you.'

'Are you serious? But what motive would I have for shooting him?'

He is calmer now, his reactions show this. But he has made a mistake.

'And how do you know he was shot?'

'You're right, I don't know...' His face is now bright red. 'I was still thinking about Zoboli...'

'Alright. You were saying...'

'I said, what motive...'

'Well you had motives... you certainly did.'

'And they are?'

'The first one is that Zanetti was about to screw you by leaving Tecnodomus suddenly. You would have been left with all the company's debts, to be paid with your own money.'

'That's your version...'

'No, it's what Katia told me just now. And she also told me she never mentioned it to you.'

'That's true...'

'Hold on. I only have Katia's word for this. But even without doubting her, you're an intelligent man, you might easily have guessed what your partner was about to do...'

'I'm sorry, but don't you realize this is a contradiction? Let's say, let's just say, that I knew... well, even killing Zanetti wouldn't have solved anything for me. I'm still the only partner left, the only one accountable...'

'Not really. In any case, you would have had your revenge. Then, with Zanetti out of the way, you would have become the sole owner of Tecnodomus. Perhaps you could have avoided the collapse of the company and improved the situation over time...'

With an ironic smirk Calabrese asks, 'And how would I have done that exactly?'

'New partners, within six months. Difficult, I know, but not impossible. Or perhaps you could have obtained a legal extension of the debts.' Cataldo waves away his objections with a gesture and signals that he has more to say. 'Everyone knows you're not Zanetti. You're independently wealthy and you have quite a different reputation to his – you're reliable. You'd be able to cover the initial debts by taking control of the company as sole proprietor. I'm no expert, but I'd say it would be worthwhile.'

'But you're forgetting about Katia.'

'As heir? No, I haven't forgotten her. Not at all. But Katia wouldn't be a problem – she knows nothing about business, she'd let you manage her interests as well. And now she's a widow, with a young child. And it makes sense that you'd want to be close to a woman who needs you, and not just because of the business. Yes, you'll have plenty of opportunity for that.' He roots through his pocket and pulls out a cigarette lighter. 'The problem, though, is something else.'

'And that is?'

'You simply can't allow anyone to discover that your incapacity isn't what it once was. Now more than ever. Life's crazy, isn't it? Now that Zanetti is dead...' There is some irony in Cataldo's voice. 'Otherwise the company that paid the compensation might ask for it back, or some of it at least. Am I right?'

'I think so.'

'I don't think so, I know so. And unfortunately this might well be another motive for killing Zanetti.'

'Are you mad?'

'Calm down, I only said it might well be a motive. Because it's just an idea, for the moment, based on the supposition that he may have known about your fake disability. Looked at that way, the motive clearly surfaces. He could have blackmailed you, for example...' and Calabrese smiles without interrupting, '... demanding you became a partner in the company. Or perhaps later, in some other form. Perhaps the payment of small sums of money every now and then... I don't know, maybe as loans or as payments from the company. I'm no expert, as I said, but I'm sure there's no shortage of ways of doing these things. And it certainly wouldn't have been the first time Zanetti had played dirty tricks.'

'He was a nasty piece of work, but he wasn't psychic.'

'Which means...?'

'Which means that you're only guessing. How did Zanetti know something that only you know and that you've only just learned?'

'Perhaps from Katia...'

'And how?'

'Let's say that you, once, misinterpreting an affectionate gesture on her part, tried to embrace her...'

He turns pale, starts shaking. Perhaps in shame, perhaps in scorn, and just like before, his voice rises, becoming even sharper this time: 'These are just imaginings, suppositions...'

'I told you that.'

'You have no proof at all!'

Cataldo gets up slowly, fatigue in his legs. 'You think if I had any proof I'd still be sitting here talking?'

Calabrese watches as he leaves, the expression on his face a mixture of a plea and sheer confusion. He does not have the courage to ask Cataldo if he will tell anyone about what he has seen.

The sun has finally set. And Cataldo thinks now, as he drives. Calabrese let him in, accepted his visit, answered the questions. And he did not ask for a lawyer, not even at the most embarrassing or tense moments... he did not even consider a lawyer, and that is a fact. And now he wonders if Calabrese had decided that to do so, suddenly, would have appeared suspicious or whether he felt himself capable of facing up to his problems on his own, or if his strength came from his own innocence. Only when Cataldo saw him get up from the wheelchair did he appear to be in difficulty –

vulnerable, unmasked. Without his secret, a secret that in the end was nothing more than unhappiness.

There is not much traffic in town. And the shadows are getting longer, stretching out. But there are other shadows that he carries within himself and they are not retreating. He is increasingly convinced, day by day, that the key to this darkness is psychological, something belonging to time gone by. Something that goes through the mind's consciousness, through one's character, and through the memories one has of the past. Because sooner or later our memories are the key to revealing things, someone had once said to him. And everyone is accountable for his or her own past. Because we all die being what we are, or what we have been.

He pulls up in Piazza Marconi, near the ice-cream kiosk. He switches off the engine. The only real proof is psychological, not material, a police officer had once said to him. For years he had believed this to be the voice of experience, but then he had discovered by chance that it came from a detective novel. But he continued to believe it, at least in part. And perhaps it was true now. Such a difficult, complicated case. A real mix too: burning passion, cool anger and sheer rancour. And hatred and envy and ambition. And then the hot summer back then, relentless, and the cold of a winter many years ago – these things came back to him. The fears, the remorse. What was that evocative phrase he had once heard and liked? Ah yes... past guilt casts long shadows. Shadows that reach the present, right up to where we are now. He chases these thoughts away, starts up the engine again. Because when we ask ourselves too many questions, we get nowhere. He looks at his watch – it is almost supper-time, but he is not hungry. And so he decides... if he is quick he will make it there, because it is nearby. Even though he has not been feeling in such good shape, as though he has the flu coming on.

The old town, the part on the hill. The convent in Via Di Vittorio. The car park is almost empty, everything is in shadow. He wonders if perhaps he has stayed late to study, whether he will find him there. He does not even put the car alarm on so as not to waste time.

He sees it straight away, as soon as he gets out. It is not in the public car park. It is parked on the right, almost up against the convent wall from which bunches of white caper flowers hang. Two wheels on the road and two on the pavement. It must have been there for some time, he says to himself, must have arrived when the car park was still full. He shakes his head, careful now, as though waiting for a revelation. Because he would never have imagined he would come across it here – the dark blue Mercedes 280S.

CHAPTER NINETEEN

Conscience

He opens the door slowly, as though worried he might disturb someone. But neither of them hear him, not even Don Lodi who is actually facing him, his head slightly bowed, listening to the other man as though hearing his confession. They are talking in low voices, more quietly than is natural, even though they are on their own. Then, when he is already in the room, Marchisio hears him and turns round. Don Lodi looks up too.

He moves closer in silence, and they both watch him without saying anything. There is a sort of reserve in the air, as though his presence – feared or undesired – is an intrusion into a private relationship. They sit there, motionless, until he pulls up a chair and sits down, his hands on the table.

'Good evening, Signori. Am I disturbing you?'

'Not in the least, Inspector. You are always welcome,' says Don Lodi, the perfect host. The other man has not said anything yet.

'I only ask because I didn't let you know I was coming...'

'Not at all,' he repeats, 'I'm sure you have good reason. Well...' and he hesitates now, 'should I introduce you?'

'No need,' says Marchisio, 'we already know each other.' And after a moment, he says to Cataldo, 'Are you surprised?'

'A bit, yes.'

'And why?'

'I didn't realize you knew each other.'

'We met this afternoon,' says Don Lodi. 'A recent acquaintance... but would you like something to drink? An aperitif?

The fridge is over there...'

'No, thank you.' He looks at his watch, it is already seven thirty. 'I won't stay long.'

'As you wish.'

The priest is cordial, but it is cordiality without warmth... distant. Marchisio on the other hand is the same as ever, just less pale because he has been in the sun a bit. It is obvious that Cataldo has interrupted something.

'Is it too much for me to ask what you were talking about?' says Cataldo suddenly.

The younger man shrugs his shoulders as though brushing the matter off or trying to avoid the question. But the priest speaks up: 'He came looking for me.' He turns to Marchisio and adds, 'You can tell him, if you want.'

'Alright.' He thinks for a moment, then begins: 'Zoboli was in that car, that night, the night that changed my life. You know that, don't you?'

'You told me.'

'And Don Lodi knew him well, everyone says that. As a student, as a person... and he'd been with Don Lodi just a few hours before...'

'So?'

'So I came here to beg him to tell me if he's learned anything over the years... at confession or through their friendship, whatever... anything regarding the second man or woman who was in that damned car...'

'Begged him to tell you...'

'Yes, to tell me. Because all I want is the truth.'

Cataldo looks at his nails. 'And the answer?'

'There has been no answer, because that's when you arrived.'

Of course, it could be the truth. It fits with Marchisio's

impulsive ingenuousness. But there remains something undefined hanging in the air, something vague, like a sort of unexpressed understanding, tacit comprehension, that renders their relationship ambiguous. And Cataldo cannot manage to wipe out that first impression, the impression that Marchisio was at confession.

'What about you, Inspector,' Don Lodi butts in, trying to be funny, 'do you have any questions for me? I must warn you that the library is about to close...'

'No, I don't. Don't worry.'

'So...'

'So why am I here?' He decides to go along with the game, to respond in the ironic tone. 'Well... since in this library...' and he looks around '... even though it's a very nice library... since you don't have a television, I thought I'd come and bring you the latest news.'

'Bad news, I imagine.'

'Why, Don Lodi?'

'If you're the messenger...'

'You're right.' Cataldo looks serious now, the joke is over. 'It's a terrible piece of news. Haven't you heard?'

Both gesture no. In the end Marchisio says: 'A death?'

'Yes, another one.' And then he adds, 'Carlo Zanetti.'

Marchisio is impassive, he does not react. But Don Lodi blurts out: 'Zanetti? Zanetti... dead?'

'Yes,' he says, and in the silence that follows he adds, '... two shots to the chest. Took place in his office, this afternoon. They're doing the post-mortem now, urgent procedure. The bullets... you understand...'

No one speaks now. Cataldo gets up, feels the tiredness in his legs, even more than before. But his brain is still working.

'Another of your pupils, Professor. And another one who was at that famous degree celebration... that damned supper, we should say...' He looks at Marchisio now. 'You used that word...'

'Me?'

'Yes, just now. But that's not the point. The point is Guiglia's going to resemble Chicago at this rate. Ever since you arrived.'

'It's not my fault.'

'We shall see.' Then he becomes sombre, speaks quietly. 'That's three now. Three dead men in four days.' He looks at Don Lodi. 'I'm thinking of Nunzio, poor soul. Did you know him?'

'I didn't,' says Marchisio. 'How could I?'

'I only knew him by sight,' murmurs the priest. 'But I hadn't seen him for a long time.'

'A long time?'

'More than a year. But I remember him. A tall man... grey hair and a wart on his nose... poor man, yes.'

'I didn't know him,' repeats Marchisio, almost as though he is afraid no one will believe him.

'An absurd crime, as well as terrible,' continues the priest. 'I read about it in the *Carlino*. But the fact he was killed in the tourist office with a paperweight from the office itself does show that it wasn't a premeditated murder.' He pauses before adding, 'Doesn't it?'

Cataldo encourages him. 'Go on.'

'If that's true, the murder might well have been the result of an argument... yes, a sudden explosion of rage after an argument.'

But Cataldo smiles.

'Is something wrong?'

'You're forgetting the time, Don Athos. He was killed ten minutes after he opened the library, and the opening was unscheduled. I found him on the floor and the murderer must have left the building just a minute or two before I arrived. See what I mean? They didn't have time to argue. No... that wasn't the motive.'

Don Lodi says nothing, he seems disappointed.

'And there's more.' He coughs, turns to face Don Lodi. 'The killer left no trace of himself. He acted quickly, struck immediately, as soon as he entered and he made sure he didn't step in the blood on the floor. And that wasn't easy... there was blood everywhere. And he took no money from the dead man's pockets.' He coughs again. 'You see? Just think about it.'

Don Lodi scratches his cheek as he thinks. Then he gives in.

'So what do you think?'

'I think we can exclude the idea of an argument, and even the idea of someone deranged – a drug addict, a madman and so on. The killer was so precise, so self-controlled, it makes me think quite differently. This was studied carefully beforehand.'

'Premeditated murder?'

'Exactly. Even if the weapon used makes us think the opposite. But the paperweight, if you think about it, tells us something. The killer knew the library and the objects in it. As well as the librarian, of course...'

'Yes. A premeditated crime, there's no doubt,' continues Cataldo after a while, without speaking to anyone in particular. 'But it's not a perfect crime. No. There's no such thing as the perfect crime.'

'That's debatable, Inspector,' says Don Lodi, very interested. Marchisio agrees, nodding his head. 'All crimes that remain unsolved are perfect crimes.'

'No.' And he looks sternly into his eyes.

'Why not?'

'Because the laws of human nature prove you wrong. You see, Don Athos, a killer's salvation is tied to an apparent lack of motive, and an alibi, of course... but even if he suffers no guilt, no remorse, just imagine the torment knowing that a single error can give him away, that if he contradicts just one of his words, or if one of his gestures gives something away... if he talks in his sleep... But let's get back to Zanetti.'

Silence returns to the room. Cataldo runs through the ideas in his mind as he walks around the table, then he makes up his mind and speaks: 'It's possible Zanetti was driving the car that night. Zoboli and Zanetti together. They're both dead.' He turns to Marchisio, suddenly, 'What would you say if that's how things were? What sort of justice has been meted out?'

'Justice would have been served twice, Inspector,' says the priest. 'Human justice and divine justice. Sometimes death exposes God's judgement on life.'

'I'm afraid I don't follow.'

He makes a gesture with his hand, as though chasing away something that is not there. 'It doesn't matter. I meant that only God knows what is right and only He can look into the hearts of men, and judge them. That's what I was telling him earlier,' and he gestures towards Marchisio, who starts a little in surprise. 'We are men and we have no right to do this.'

'I don't agree with you. Crime always requires judgement, a sentence. Here and now, whatever the motive. God comes later.'

'Don't you think that...'

'No. Let's be realistic, please. Revenge isn't justice.'

A shadow of surprise seems to pass over the priest's eyes, almost disappointed that he finds no understanding from Cataldo. But he says nothing. He takes off his glasses, sighs deeply, then he puts them back on, almost as though the gesture were a nervous tic. Cataldo turns to the other man.

'It's your turn now. Where were you this afternoon, between one and three o'clock?'

Marchisio is calm, precise, almost as if he has been expecting this. 'I had lunch in the hotel. But between midday and half past one, I think. I finished at a quarter to two at the latest.'

'And then?'

'I went to my room, to rest.'

'You didn't go out to carry on with your investigation?'

He does not smile. 'No. It was too hot.'

'But that's the second time this has happened.'

'That what has happened?'

'That you don't have an alibi. The same thing happened with Zoboli...'

'I remember.'

Silence, again. And Cataldo thinks it is as though they are all breathing quietly, so as not to break the silence. He turns his back on them, walks towards a window and looks out. He wants to open it even though it is cool in the room. He is just doing this when Marchisio speaks.

'I'm going back home tomorrow.'

Two faces turn to him – concerned, confused. But it is Cataldo who asks, 'Tomorrow?'

'Yes, tomorrow. I just have to collect some photographs I've had developed in Modena.'

'What photos?'

He does not answer. 'Or do I have to stay here?'

'What do you think?' A pause. 'Are you involved in these crimes somehow?'

And Marchisio looks at Cataldo in the great silence that has developed. Then he says, slowly, 'We're all involved, Inspector. In all the crimes in the world.'

'That's not an answer!' He loses his patience, raises his voice. 'Those are just fine words. Or maybe a line from a TV cop show.'

'It's not my fault if you don't like it.' It is odd that there is no irony in his voice. 'But I don't know what else to say. Really.'

So Cataldo puts his chair back in its place and stands, his hands on the back of it. After a while he takes his leave of the priest with a nod, then looks at Marchisio for some time, undecided. In the end he asks him the last question, even though he knows it is pointless.

'Tell me one thing at least. Just one. Is everything cleared up now?'

His voice is calm, peaceful. And the eyes that look back at him seem sincere.

'No one can ever fully clear his conscience.'

But what is conscience? thinks Cataldo a few minutes later as he is leaving. Nothing more than a polite name, someone said once, for superstition. Which in its turn is a euphemism for fear.

He is perturbed as he gets into his car. And as he drives his worry grows, like an autumn shadow. Because he knows well that there is always, in every case, a difficult moment in which ambiguity, the stumbling block of appearances, people's reticence, make solving the mystery seem more complicated, if not impossible. And this is one of those moments.

What was Marchisio doing there? Did he already know Don Lodi? Because in the end, when you go looking for a priest you do it out of penitence, out of remorse, or out of faith that gives hope. Was that what was going on? And why now, why throughout this case, has he been left with the feeling that something is escaping him? Something he felt clearly today... but what is it? And who is it? And why does he still have two or three sentences in his head that he cannot make sense of? His own impatience takes him by surprise in the very moment in which he recognizes it. He is on edge, yes. He is even angry with himself. Perhaps it is the heat, perhaps he really is worn out. He concentrates on the road now because he is at a crossroads and he has to turn.

Three dead men in four days, he had just said that. Including Nunzio, the unluckiest of them all, killed when he was just moments away from being safe. He feels anxious, but he knows he cannot afford to be. And it does not make sense to talk of a lack of luck, which is just a way of consoling ourselves for a lack of efficiency. He has to remain calm, that is all there is to it. He has to rationalize the tension, the anxiety. Time is not slipping away – he has done everything he could do up to now.

So, if Marchisio has nothing more to do in Guiglia, and if Zoboli and Zanetti really were the culprits that night back in 1980, then yes, it is clear how Zanetti found the money to buy into Tecnodomus. And not just that, it is also clear that Marchisio understood all this too, and so, out of revenge... he knows all the rest.

Yes, everything makes sense now. Or almost everything. Because if this idea is correct, if the two of them really were together in the car, well... looking back over the whole enquiry, it is clear someone has been lying to him. And now he knows exactly who it is. He just hopes she is at home.

CHAPTER TWENTY

Two women

'So you were driving that night?' Cataldo looks at her, almost mockingly.

She lifts her head on hearing the question. She is sitting in an armchair, her face inexpressive and an obstinate turn to her lips, together with a vague anxiety in her eyes. She nods, without speaking. And he thinks to himself that there really is something admirable in her tenacity. So he waits for a second before continuing, emphasizing every single word: 'What time did you say you left with him?'

Her expression does not change, but her eyes widen: 'At eleven o'clock.'

'And you went home?'

'Yes...'

'That's not true,' he replies, firmly.

'What did you say?'

She looks down and looks agitated while she becomes more rigid, pulling in her elbows as her breathing speeds up involuntarily.

'God knows you're lying.'

She lifts her head with a start. The blood has left her face and her rosy cheeks look like unnatural marks on her pale skin.

'How dare you...'

But he blocks her reaction simply by lifting his hand. Miriam understands now and she begins to relax.

'What makes you think that I...?' she starts to ask, without conviction. Her voice is colourless now, but Cataldo understands the tone, the question.

'Because I know.'

It is the end of the waiting, of the deceit. The words that follow will be the truth.

'No, you're right.' She blows her nose, without crying. 'There's something I didn't tell you.'

'Giulio wasn't with you?'

'That's right.'

'What about the others, they confirmed it?'

She shakes her head. 'They're not involved. They really did see us get in the car together and leave...'

'And then?'

'Then I understood...'

'What?'

'That he wanted to end the party in a motel. He wanted to let off steam with me... on top of me... all his resentment, his jealousy... just to forget it all.' She speaks quickly, almost mumbling. 'But I understood...'

'That there was no love in his arousal. It was just tension, and anger.'

'Yes.'

He does not tell her that Calabrese, the sharpest of them all, was right: all that drinking was not merriment, it was envy, rancour. Rancour for the person who had used him, many times, the person who was being fêted that night...

'So what did you do?'

'I said no, I got out of the car. I walked away.'

'Alone?'

'Yes.'

'In the dark?'

'I know how to look after myself.'

'I'm sure you do.' He looks at her with respect, 'And

Giulio?'

'I don't know... I only know that he turned the car around and went back, after throwing insults at me. He was out of his head and I was worried about him...' And in a quieter voice, a whisper, she adds, 'I think he went back to the party.'

And then he left later, thinks Cataldo, this time with Zanetti. And they took the same road.

'At eleven o'clock?'

'Shortly afterwards then, yes. I wasn't lying about the time.'

At least about that, he says to himself.

She cries quietly now, making no sound, her hands gripping the glass, the glass that he has filled for her and put in her hand before lighting a cigarette for himself. Her eyes are red, her face swollen. And her voice is a bit hoarse when she finds the strength to speak.

'Do you think that Giulio... you think he took the money that night?'

She looks like a child now, naming a fear to defeat it: 'Tell me... is that what you think?'

Cataldo is silent for a while. Then he says, 'I think so.'

A sudden painful grimace adds years to her face. 'No, I don't believe it. It's not possible. If you'd met him, you wouldn't believe it either... he wasn't a bad man, really he wasn't. There are some things a wife just knows...'

In her heart, quite. In her heart she was sure. But what does a heart know of the complexity of a man? Of that mixture of love and iniquity that we all carry around inside? But he does not say this.

'You loved him very much, didn't you?'

She does not need to answer, even an idiot would have

known. But she does, 'Love is what's left when you take all the selfishness away. And I had a lot to give him.'

He looks at her with understanding. He knows that is the way things are. Between a man and a woman there is a bit of all of this – love and selfishness, desire and tenderness, altruism and fidelity, and then esteem, jealousy, passion... but he also knows that Calabrese was right again: we do not control the duration of a love, or the duration of our lives.

'Do you miss him so much? To the point of denying the evidence?'

This time she does not reply. And so he gives her time, out of sympathy.

'Perhaps you're right. The death of a loved one always leaves a void.'

'A void, yes,' he reflects. 'A void that can only be filled with memories and nostalgia. Because death is always mysterious.'

That is it. He is about to leave, then he stops, his hand on the door handle.

'There's one more thing I have to ask you.' He hesitates a moment. 'It's not pleasant.'

'Go on.'

'Did your husband have a lover?'

She lowers her head, without replying. Perhaps she is crying silently, like before. She sits like that for a long time. And now it does not matter if she says she does not know. Which is exactly what she does, without lifting her face.

'I don't know. Believe me, I don't know.' She coughs, then adds, 'Perhaps he did, but it wasn't important. What mattered was that he was here for me. That he dedicated time to being with me...'

He nods and leaves, walks outside into the cool of an

approaching storm that may break soon. He leans on the car door, thinking. The crossroads of lives that are tied together, lives that deceive one another, lose one another, find one another again, or not. Lives that succumb to the temptation to live, or to die. And the mystery that follows every love story. Because one life, one love is not enough to use up a person completely. But Miriam really did love her man, whatever he was. And perhaps she has not lost everything if she is left with the bitter privilege of shedding tears for him.

Cataldo himself has lost more. A vision flashes through his mind, suddenly, as he gets into the car and waits. Perhaps it was the fresh air, or Miriam's eyes that brought it back to him. That time at Ognina, in the autumn. Evening, the sea was grey with white flecks of small, breaking waves. The beach was far away, beyond the rocks, fading into an infinite blue. There was a great silence all around him and Tina, sitting close, watching the water. Suddenly they looked at each other and his breath came more quickly, his desire, intense, rose to his eyes and he wanted to hold her, but she had pulled away, a slight gesture, but an unequivocal one. 'Why?' he had asked, gently. There was no resentment, because it was simply that she could not fake love. That was the moment in which they told each other the truth. It was fatal... necessary. No one to blame. By then it was too late to change anything.

That had been the last time. She had gone to the car while he sat there watching her disappear. From his life. Then night had fallen suddenly, the way darkness does on a winter's day.

He told himself sometimes that he had been unjust, selfish. That he had not really wanted her, that he had chosen not to do anything about it – he could have run after her, stopped her, he could have gone back to look for her. That is what he told himself. But then he thought that she had not really loved him enough, she had loved him less than she loved her parents, her habits, the life she led. And only later had he understood that no one can teach us what to do in the moment of farewell.

Every time he thinks he has forgotten about it, it all comes back. Like now. Especially at sunset, in the silence, like the last time he saw her. While the white walls turn dirty with the shadows.

CHAPTER TWENTY-ONE

The arrest

He waits a little longer before calling Muliere on his mobile.

'Well? Everything set with Petronio?'

'Yes, Inspector, no problem. He signed it straight away, I've got it with me. I didn't even have to ask twice.'

Just as well, he thinks – he knows that his deputy's energy is inversely proportionate to his eloquence.

From the receiver comes a faint hoarseness, the usual voice, 'So... this evening then?'

'Yes, but don't worry, there's no rush. Take your time and have something to eat. Let's make it...' and he raises his left wrist to look at his watch, '... say, in two hours' time. At eleven. And bring someone with you... whoever's available, as long as he's on the ball.'

'Three of us then. Okay.'

'There shouldn't be any trouble, but you never know...'

He puts his mobile away and thinks for a while, his face marked by the lines that always appear when he is troubled. Then he returns to the car, gets in and looks out through the half-open window. Outside now, the air on the road carries the smell of the countryside, and the sky has turned a dark blue. But the wind is getting up and he shivers slightly.

They find the pistol almost immediately in Marchisio's hotel room, wrapped in a towel at the bottom of the wardrobe. Muliere is holding it now in a rather strange way – with a pencil through the trigger guard. 'It's been fired recently,' he says, looking at it thoughtfully. Then he turns to Marchisio and says, 'Should've thrown it away.'

Marchisio moves closer and he too looks at the Beretta, then he frowns and the shadows under his eyes darken. 'It's not mine,' he says in the end, his voice hoarse.

'Come on, Marchisio. You're nailed now: pistol, motive, everything,' says Muliere, more on edge than usual since he knelt down to look under the bed and got up with his face all red. 'So... like to tell us all about it then?'

'It's not mine, I tell you! It's the first time I've seen it.'

'Things aren't looking good for you. Don't you understand?' Cataldo says, less sharply. 'Don't you want to make a statement?'

'You honestly think I used that?'

'What I think doesn't come into it. You well know it's all up to the investigating judges, the prosecutors, defence lawyers, experts and so on... so?'

He seems confused as he looks first at Muliere, then at Cataldo, and he lifts a hand to his mouth.

'Was it you, then?'

His mouth is shut tight. His eyes are closed. He shakes his head several times, slowly. Then he opens his eyes and turns to Cataldo, who asked the question.

'No, no. I've never seen it before...' But his voice is cracking.

Cataldo shakes his head. 'It's pointless, carrying on like this. Denying the evidence.' And then, almost under his breath, he says to Muliere, 'To tell you the truth, I really didn't imagine we'd find it here.'

Marchisio grabs at these words: 'But it's the truth. That pistol isn't mine, how many times do I have to tell you!'

'So how come it was in your wardrobe? Eh?'

'I'm innocent, I didn't fire it, I didn't kill anyone...' He has blurted all this out in one breath, his face red, then he swallows and adds, 'It's just like back then, eighteen years ago...'

'Answer the bloody question!'

Cataldo has raised his voice for a moment and it is full of pain and rage.

'Someone planted it...' Marchisio says, swallowing before he continues, 'Someone wants to set me up...'

'Just like back then... we understand,' says Muliere. 'We'll take him in now, won't we?'

'Straight away, yes. To Petronio.'

'You'd best get dressed,' says the third policeman, silent up till now.

While Marchisio gets changed, in silence now, Cataldo opens the windows and looks out. Under the porticoes, people are walking, chatting, but no one looks up towards them and through another open window in the hotel he can hear a television.

He turns back around and everything is ready. The Beretta is in a plastic bag, Marchisio is dressed, not wearing handcuffs, standing there between Muliere and the other officer. He starts proclaiming his innocence again, blurting it out now and then in the same words and Cataldo gives him one last look as they lead him away. He suddenly notices a purplish mark on Marchisio's right cheek, as though he had caught a chill from a cold wind, and the dark circles of sweat in the armpits of his cream-coloured shirt. He feels almost sorry for him.

They go out of the hotel into a moonless night. The sky is dark, flecked with grey clouds. And the cool air still carries the smell of damp soil.

CHAPTER TWENTY-TWO

The photograph

The shutters in his bedroom are closed, but the windows are open. The air still carries the smell of soil, just like in the countryside after a storm. But there has been no storm yet.

Cataldo cannot get to sleep. And it is not because of the cool air, the damp. It is because now and then some sediment of unease, of painful embarrassment resurfaces. That is when he scratches his nose, thoughtfully, with his thumb and his index finger.

Marchisio is inside. No alibi, no defence, caught with the pistol almost in his hand. So? It is all over, isn't it? So why is he still looking for something?

There is a black void inside him – deep and sad. He has no desire to switch on the television, to seek a distraction. The flickering bluish light, at moments like this, just seems to underline his solitude, his melancholy. Because there are moments, in a case, that bring with them a feeling of uselessness, of inefficiency – when there is a sense of bitterness, of worry that rises and that then in the end you manage to chase away. Sometimes a memory is enough to save you, to save someone else. To pull you out of the storm.

And it is a memory, yes... it is a detail. Something important that had struck him, but now he cannot bring it into focus... or is it just an impression, is he the one who is making a mistake? Or is it time? Perhaps it is time itself that is changing, making him so unsettled, so reluctant to accept the end?

Or is it something else? Something that is moving in the

depths of his memory, something living that demands to surface, to be seen by everyone. If only he could help it along. Zoboli, Zanetti, Marchisio, and then the pistol... has this story not ended a bit too neatly? Don't the pieces fit together into a shape that is just too obvious? And that photograph?

He throws the sheet off the bed. He sighs. Then he starts thinking again, his ears soaking up the silence, his back resting on the pillow, leaning on the headboard. He insists on remembering, on sifting out of these past days' work all the objects, the words, all the things that are clinging to his patience. Because he knows, he knows very well, that perception is guided by expectations and that we always see, even if we would rather not, what we expect to see, what we believe in. But instead he has to remember and nothing more, without exerting any influence from his own logic, or his own imagination. All this even though there is the way things happen, and the way we remember them.

But it is difficult now. It would almost be better to get up, to do something. He picks up a book and goes into the kitchen to smoke. Or maybe to put on a tape of Franco Battiato's songs, the one with *Gli Uccelli*, which always calms him down, and leads him to lose himself in the emotive crescendo of its melody. But there would not be any point, it would not cure his unease. So it is best to go and wait in bed. To think.

Then, slowly, all the hints begin to condense into precise images. And even he does not know exactly when, he will never know, but in the end it comes back to him – clear, correct, that something, the string that when pulled unravels all his thoughts. So he smiles to himself in the half-light, switches off the bedside lamp and lies down, satisfied, while outside it sounds as though it is beginning to rain. He is at peace now, there is no hurry. He will go tomorrow to check it out. And the rain will be good for the land, after all that heat.

He opens the window and looks out. The light is bluish, there is a dirty grey colour hanging over the roads and the sky, clinging to the houses. He has never had so much to do on a Saturday morning. He makes the first phone call still in his underpants.

'Good morning, Inspector... the results? Of course... they said they'd be ready by nine.'

'Do you know if they've actually worked on it?'

'Oh yes... last night. Urgent... Petronio told them.'

'Good. I'm on my way.'

It is drizzling over Guiglia and the sky is like a dirty sheet. He has gone to the bathroom to wash his face and now his eyes feel prickly. And he feels it immediately, like a premonition, that subtle unhappiness that waking up leaves in one's mouth.

It is raining harder now, out on the road. There is almost no one around – a few open umbrellas, silence in the car. The dull rhythm of the water on the bodywork, the rumble of an engine now and then, and the spray from the wheels. And out of town the horizon is a combination of the grey of the tarmac and the grey of the sky.

Quarter past nine, his third coffee. From the machine in the corridor.

'The post-mortem results are in. And the forensic report.'

The voice behind him takes him by surprise. Even though he knows who it is.

'I've put everything on your desk.'

'Haven't you had a look?'

'Yes, of course. You know...'

'And?'

'Just as we imagined.'

Muliere's face is relaxed, Cataldo knows him well. He is always like this at the end of a case.

They go into the office together. Cataldo points to the papers.

'Have they already been sent to Petronio?'

The other man raises his arms, a bit pathetically: 'I don't know.'

'Doesn't matter. Let's see...'

He sits down and starts reading quietly. Everything fits. The two bullets that killed Zanetti were shot by the same Beretta that killed Zoboli, and the weapon is the one found in Marchisio's room.

'Crystal clear, isn't it?'

'No.'

The Inspector's frown wipes the contented smile from his deputy's face.

'Why not?'

'Read this.'

Muliere, opposite him, plants his elbows on the table and cranes his neck.

'Down here. No fingerprints on Marchisio's pistol. Nothing.'

Outside, the heavy rain has stopped, now it is just a diffuse whisper.

By the time they get in the car, the rain has stopped altogether; there is a poster hanging from the wall of the town hall. Cataldo notices it as he drives past, pulling up to park on the hill, just before that narrow lane from where it is difficult to see the heavens. Everything is just like the day before. The buzz of the intercom, the click of the door, the smell of mould. And he is there on the second floor, standing in front of the open door.

'Are you looking for me?'

'Yes. For the last time.' And since he does not move, Cataldo adds, 'Didn't I tell you I'd be back?'

'Yes, perhaps you did.' He moves, finally, to let him in. 'Perhaps you're right.' The professor is pale, he looks exhausted, but he says, 'So you've cracked it?'

'I believe so.'

He stops suddenly, in the entrance.

'But Marchisio...'

'We've arrested him. But you know that too.'

'So?'

'So what do I want here? Is that what you're asking?'

'Yes! Exactly! Why can't you just let me be?'

He is so on edge that it is difficult for Cataldo not to let himself be infected with his anxiety. But one quick look makes the academic stop in his tracks, brings him back to the minimum of politeness: 'I'm sorry,' he whispers.

'Don't worry. But tell me, why are you so wound up?'

'I'm not wound up...'

'What are you afraid of, then?'

'Who, me?'

Because fear is easy to read, in so many small signs: the trembling fingers, the tension rising in the voice. And the way he holds his gaze, with an air of challenge and defiant patience. He will relax in a moment.

'Good for you.'

He goes into the living room and looks around. 'Are you on

your own?'

'Yes. Why?'

'No reason.'

Cataldo smiles now. And before the other man can ask him why, he carries on speaking, but his voice is different now – calm, peaceful.

'Sometimes an object enters into your life and it just doesn't want to leave it... remember I told you that?'

'Yes... I think so.'

'Well... for me it's a photograph. The same one.' He looks at Ramondini again, smiles again. 'Understand now? I'd like to see those photographs, the ones we looked at yesterday. Just for a moment, to be sure of something.'

He is amazed. 'Is that all?'

Cataldo nods. 'Could you get them, please?'

He walks away and comes back with the old-fashioned album in its floral cover. Cataldo picks it up, opens it, but patiently because he already knows what he is looking for. It is just the one photograph that interests him and he finds it immediately – towards the end. So he stops turning the pages and hands the open album to the other man.

'This one.'

Ramondini looks at it, his eyes wide open... curious. Then he starts looking more closely. For a moment it is as though he is trying to understand something very important, some great mystery of life. Then his expression opens and Cataldo understands that Ramondini has realized who the killer is, now knows the name of the person who entered that dark, evil place with Zoboli.

He takes back the album, pulls the photograph from the cellophane pocket, and places the album on the table.

'May I?'

'Sorry? Oh... yes, of course.'

Then Cataldo sighs, tapping his index finger on the photo.

'I should have realized yesterday,' he says, sombre. Because out of disorder there has come harmony. It is clear now, now he knows.

CHAPTER TWENTY-THREE

The truth

He seems lost now, confused. All his authority has vanished, and this happened even before Cataldo pulled the photograph out.

'It's all over.' And after a moment's pause: 'You do realize, don't you, why I've come?'

He says nothing. He really is lost in some far off world.

So Cataldo shows him the photograph, the one he took from Ramondini. He does not even look at it, but all of a sudden, he responds: 'They told me you were good at your job.'

Cataldo keeps his guard up: 'I simply used my eyes. Tried to be objective.'

Who said that in life everything happens in a moment, and that a photograph can take that moment and make it eternal? That is exactly what has happened here. And there is a destiny tied to this photograph.

He is motionless there in front of him, and the light on the desk illuminates the upper part of his face, leaving his chin and his mouth in shadow. A muscle near the outer corner of his left eye contracts spasmodically.

Cataldo is relentless, handing him the photo. And perhaps, who knows, he will remember for a long time the sight of those screwed up eyes, trying to focus, and the big hand. And then his own voice: 'You see, everything has a story to tell. A letter... even a photograph, can be misinterpreted, but they never lie. It's human beings who do that.' He stares at him, changes his tone, 'Just as you've done.'

208

The other man nods, surrenders. No resistance. And he looks at Cataldo through his tired eyes.

'You knew I wouldn't deny the truth. Yes, you knew,' he says quietly, his voice full of fatigue. Now he looks beyond Cataldo, without seeing anything. Not even the oak bookshelves with their attractive inlaid decoration, the ivory bindings of the books. He is trapped in the tension.

Now Cataldo looks at the photo too. The killer is face to face with Ramondini in the picture, as they raise their glasses in a toast, perhaps the last one of the evening because there is a waiter already clearing the table...

'There's a clock on the wall... it's clearer in other photos. See? It's very small here, almost in the corner,' adds Cataldo. 'If the photographer had moved just a little it would have disappeared. I only mention that because I'm sure if it's enlarged properly we'll be able to read the time. But that's not important... the clock doesn't matter. The waiter was enough to make me realize...'

The other man lowers his head and Cataldo continues, 'that you weren't the first to leave, to get ready for the next day's conference on Rebora. Sometimes you don't need answers, you just have to ask yourself the right questions. Then the answers come along by themselves.'

He swallows, takes a deep breath, then adds: 'So I asked myself why you might lie about this... and with such detail. There was no apparent reason for it. But often what logically appears irrational leads straight to the truth.'

Now Cataldo's voice is cold, cutting. Merciless.

'You killed Nunzio for this photo. For nothing.'

Don Lodi lifts his eyes, and it seems to cost him an incredible effort. And when he speaks his voice is unrecognizable.

'I realized almost immediately... after I told you... that I shouldn't have been so precise about the time, because I remembered Nunzio and his magazine. So I checked in the library...'

'Where?'

'Not here. In Modena.'

'At the Estense?'

'Yes...'

'Ah... carry on.'

'I saw the photograph...'

'And you took it.'

'Yes.' He hesitates before adding, 'With a razor blade. There's never much surveillance in the private study room...'

'Reserved for scholars, eh? And then?'

'Then I had to destroy the other photo that certainly existed, the one here in Guiglia...'

For a moment Cataldo's voice quavers, 'And to think that it was my fault too... I'd spoken to Nunzio about it.'

'You only mentioned it, but I realized that you were going to go and look for it, so I had to get there before you...' He pauses anxiously. 'But I didn't want to kill him... no, not him. I only wanted the photograph.'

'Go on.'

'Then I saw the paperweight, on the table, near the open book, the issues of *Guiglia Oggi*... I only wanted to steal the photo, to tear it out of the page without killing anyone... that was how I wanted to make it disappear and no one would have known how long it had been missing... or perhaps they'd never have found out... but that wasn't possible anymore. And then I saw the paperweight... the paperweight. The thought came to me that people would think the crime wasn't premeditated... I didn't know you were on your way.'

'I should have realized last night,' Cataldo grumbles.

'How?' asks the priest. But he is so tired it is obvious he has no real interest in the answer.

'From a mistake that you made. When you mentioned that wart on his nose. Nunzio didn't have a wart, he'd never had one. In the half-light of the tourist office you mistook a match burn for a wart – Nunzio had a small accident on Wednesday morning. Nothing wrong with that, but you couldn't have seen him a year ago, as you claimed, with that sore on his nose, it must have been a few days ago at the most. And we both know precisely which day you saw him...'

He looks at Cataldo, almost as though imploring him: 'There is... there has to be a dark side to every man in which his will is almost impotent. You must believe me... there's something inside him that a man's will just cannot control...'

Cataldo stops him with a gesture: 'Let's forget the dark side of man. Tell me what happened that night eighteen years ago. I think it's about time.'

Don Lodi points to himself in the photograph, very different from how he is now – an exhausted old man.

'I remember there was one last toast. I said goodbye to Ramondini at almost midnight. And then I got in the car with Zoboli. He'd come back, he'd started drinking again and he was so drunk I felt sorry for him. He had ruined the evening for everyone with all his envy. And that stupid woman Miriam wasn't around when he really needed her...'

He coughs, turns red in the face, and when he starts again his voice is hoarser. 'I couldn't let him leave in that state. So I drove. But I was on edge, worried... perhaps I was driving too fast, I don't know... and it was raining and at the Torre bend we met the Mercedes, and it went off the road.'

He has said all this in one single breath and now he swallows.

'And then?'

'I turned the car round and went back. I should have recognized the driver, but I didn't... all that blood. There was blood everywhere – on his face, his neck – his head had smashed against the windscreen. But he was still alive. Perhaps we could have done something...'

'But then you saw the money.'

'Yes. Lots of it all over the back seat – the suitcase had sprung open. We stood there staring, looking at him and then we looked each other in the eye... I've always thought that at that moment Zoboli had suddenly sobered up, that he was suddenly back with us...'

'So then what did you do?'

'Nothing. We just stood there in the cold for ages, while he struggled for breath, moaning, more and more quietly, his eyes closed. Just towards the end I think he opened them, looked at me, but maybe it was just nerves... then we realized he was dead.'

'Just a minute. Let me get this straight. You stood there side by side watching him die?'

He has spoken quietly, calmly, but inside there is a repressed anger that gives his words remarkable force. The other man nods.

'But it wasn't our fault, it was just fate... pure chance. If Giulio hadn't been drinking, if we hadn't taken that road...'

He is about to say that we create our own fate, but then he thinks better of it. What does it matter now anyway?

'And then?'

'We just took the money in the dark, without saying a

word. And we agreed we wouldn't spend it for a while, until things had calmed down. We didn't even know there had been two of them in the car. And when we did find out, it was too late...'

'It wasn't too late.'

Cataldo's voice, even though controlled, expresses his anger: 'There was a young man doing time. But forget that, just carry on... or shall I do it? Once the trial was over, Zoboli got married and bought the villa... and you? You tell me, because I'd like to understand...'

'I gave up teaching to set up the publishing house. Then the Foundation... my dream come true.' He nods now, as though speaking to himself. 'Yes, that's how it was. Everyone needs dreams. To give up on your dreams means you never grow up... often it's just another way of dying...'

Cataldo's gaze becomes severe as the priest continues monotonously: 'That's where the difference is. Ordinary people have careers, make money, nurture mediocre loves... but they never have the courage to take their own dreams seriously.'

'These aren't dreams, Don Lodi. These are ambitions! And ambition isn't love for your fellow man, it's self-love... egotism. That's what it is.' And he stares into Don Lodi's eyes severely and the other man holds his gaze for a moment, then turns his head to the floor, to an imaginary point by his feet. 'Ambition is a cancer. If it grows, it dominates your will and then it destroys you.'

Don Lodi continues speaking, almost as if he has not heard. 'It was my dream, yes. My life's dream. A man is alive for as long as his dreams are alive.' And he turns to Cataldo: 'Do you have a dream?'

'Yes. To be a normal person. Capable of sympathizing with

other people's pain. But then I realize, as I do now, just how inadequate we all are in life, and in death too.'

There is a deep silence now, and Cataldo respects it. He has looked at his watch just once since they started, but decided that Petronio can wait. Because there is still something he would like to know, and perhaps it will come now as the priest starts talking again.

'Eighteen years ago I really believed. You watch a man die, you wait until he exists no more. He has become a thing. Nothing. He exists no longer, not even his mind... I really did believe it. I thought that the years would have diluted all the turmoil into some sort of detachment, that the memory would eventually be free of remorse...' He stops, lifts a hand to his shirt collar: 'I thought the memory of that night would have hovered for a while near that black hole into which everything disappears suddenly, painlessly, creating the illusion of a time in which we never existed.' His breathing is strange now, almost asthmatic, but he continues: 'I believed this. But no. It's not easy to exorcize remorse... or to make a compromise with guilt. Because you can't change what you've done, and even if you try there's always something that will carry you back again. Because the anguish returned with Marchisio's arrival. And I had to do it. I killed Zoboli first, at his house.'

'Why?'

'He'd called me. He wanted to settle things with Marchisio, who'd been to see him. I didn't know what to do, but I took my pistol. Then Zoboli pulled his pistol out to show it to me, he'd already made up his mind about what to do. So then I made mine up.'

'The same type of gun...'

'Identical. He'd copied me. I bought mine first... a long

time ago.'

'Alright, alright. But why in his right temple?'

'It was a sudden idea that came to me. It might make them think it was a stranger... that's why I shot him there.'

Cataldo nods. 'But that's exactly what made me suspicious. No one commits a crime that goes against their character. And there was an intelligence behind this crime. A criminal mind. Just like yours.'

He pulls a cigarette out of his packet, but he does not light it.

'Do you remember when I told you that the perfect crime doesn't exist? Even you made a mistake... three in fact.'

The other man looks at him, but with no curiosity.

'First, when someone shoots himself the direction taken by the bullet is usually upwards, not downward. Second, on the hand that pulls the trigger there are always traces of smoke or powder, and there was neither on Zoboli's. Third, you should have realized that the microscope analysis would show categorically that Zoboli's Beretta hadn't fired the bullet into his head.'

'I thought everyone would immediately think it had been suicide.'

'And that the enquiry would stop there?'

'Yes.'

'Now I know what you did then. You put on a pair of gloves, you took Zoboli's pistol, with his prints on it, and you placed it close to his head, after having fired a shot from it. Am I right?'

'Yes, out the window at the back, towards the country-side... I took my pistol with me.'

'And then you used it again. On Zanetti.' He looks at him now as he pulls out his lighter and adds, 'Zanetti... why?'

'Can't you guess?' He smiles slightly, bitterly.

He is right, it is not difficult to guess: 'Blackmail?'

Athos Lodi speaks even more slowly now, with concentration. Is it repentance, or is it just undone pride?

'Zanetti, a long time after the event, remembered what really happened. Zoboli had left with Miriam, but then came back on his own. He left with me, at the end of the evening. Idiot... all he was good for was selling one apartment a year.'

Cataldo wants to laugh, but all that comes is a strange, suffocated sound.

'But he managed to remember me almost twenty years after that night...' he says bitterly. 'He phoned me the day before yesterday, while everyone was here...'

'Then you cleaned the pistol and planted it in Marchisio's room. You must have done that last night, while he was eating, since you knew that he planned to leave today.'

'I had no choice. At that stage...'

'But even there I got suspicious, when we found the pistol with no prints. It's called the utility of anomalies, just as they taught us in police college. Think about it. Someone kills two people with a gun, but he doesn't throw it away, he actually cleans it and puts it away in his wardrobe... but why if he'd already completed his act of revenge? And so that was a help, too, in understanding what happened.

'And then there was another thing, last night,' Cataldo continues, calmly. 'When you said that there are things we have no right to judge... and then you added... what was it you said? Ah.... yes, "I was telling him just before..." and you were referring to Marchisio, who was sitting here. Remember? You gave me the impression that he had come to confession, looking for some sort of absolution from you...

but that couldn't have been the reason for his visit. Marchisio never thought of himself, not even indirectly, as some sort of avenger. You wanted to raise this suspicion, channelling my thoughts in his direction.'

Looking at him now, it seems impossible to imagine that this tired old man, stripped of his charisma, has killed, and killed again, with a perverse consistency, with a precise wilfulness. The will to eliminate, to silence. And Cataldo almost wants to ask him if the money has brought him the good life he had dreamed of. If the publishing house and the Foundation and all the rest were really worth that much to him. But there is no time for all this, he has to tell him to stand up. Because it is all over.

'It's funny, though,' he whispers, 'that it was a photograph that made you realize.'

'Evidence. Today we'll be doing the stub test.'

'What's that?' There is a vague look of worry in his eyes.

'A pad swipe. It picks up traces of gunpowder on the hand. The last time you used the gun was yesterday afternoon. And even if you were wearing gloves we'll find something on your arm, on your face, on the clothes you were wearing.' He takes a deep breath, reflects for a moment. 'And maybe someone will have seen you last night at the Bandieri. A bit of a strange place for a priest to be...'

He does not mention the tape recorder he is carrying in his pocket, a Sony 30x45 that he switched on at the beginning of their conversation, something he has done in other cases.

'It doesn't matter. You knew I wouldn't have denied it,' he says, tiredly. 'Perhaps it's just as well it's all over...'

Cataldo had hoped it would happen like this. He could not imagine Don Lodi reacting dramatically, attempting to escape... his face pressed to the floor, the cuffs on his wrists behind his back...

'Yes, it's just as well it's over. For too many years I've loved a god who is not God... my god has been writing, publishing, managing other people's writing, other people's thoughts... a passion no less absorbing than faith.'

A slight smile seems to cross his lips. And so Cataldo says, 'Ambition is a character flaw. I told you. Often our flaws are simply virtues that have got out of control.'

They look each other in the eye, without speaking, as they listen to the noise of the rain falling. It has started again, but it is just a quiet murmur.

And after a while the priest says, simply, 'I'm sorry about Nunzio, about the others. It was absurd, cruel. But it wasn't me who did it...'

And since Cataldo obviously does not understand, he adds, 'No, it wasn't me. It was fear.'

Who once said that men believe they are free only because they know nothing of the forces that govern their lives?

'When I was young and at university,' he seems to change the subject, suddenly, but he has not, 'I studied archaeology. Christian archaeology... I chose to major in it. Well... what I wanted to say is that you would have been a good archaeologist. You have a gift for bringing the past to life. And each of us is responsible for our own past. But none of this matters now...'

He stands up, looks straight ahead. And the only thing expressed in his eyes is resignation. Then he looks at Cataldo.

'You're very intelligent,' he says.

Cataldo thinks of Goethe, who thought that true kindness is the highest form of human intelligence.

Muliere and another officer, the same one who was there at the arrest last night, are in the unmarked car on the other side of the road, opposite the convent. The windscreen wipers are on, the tarmac is a black mirror.

Don Lodi is at the door with Cataldo behind him. Just a moment ago he looked at the library for the last time, the reading room, the brass plaque carrying the name of the Foundation. The Foundation that had been his dream. Who knows if he will ever come to think of himself as someone who dreamed the wrong dreams.

Now everything seems normal – his black jacket, his grey hat. He looks ready for a walk, except that it is raining and he does not have an umbrella. Only when they are on the pavement does he seem to have some doubt, which comes to him perhaps because people are passing by, talking to one another.

'Inspector, are you coming as well?'

Cataldo shakes his head, twice.

Don Lodi puts his hand in his pocket and pulls something out in his clenched fist, which he then extends towards Cataldo, who does not understand but takes the object. And then, with no more hesitation, Don Lodi crosses the road alone towards the waiting car.

Muliere is at the steering wheel and he raises his left hand to signal to Cataldo that everything is alright, while the other officer gets out and opens one of the rear doors for the priest. Then the car slides away on the shiny tarmac. None of them turn to look out the car windows as they disappear.

Cataldo is back in the library now, looking out of the windows through the rain. He should be in his office, writing up his report. But he does not want to go, his mind is full of thoughts... he does not know, for example, what he is meant to do with the key. The key that the priest put in his hand. Perhaps in the end he will just give it to Petronio, let him sort it out. Yes, that is what he will do. That is the best thing. Let the past bury its dead, he had said to Marchisio the first time he met him. Yes, that is what he said a century ago. And Marchisio had not listened, and he had been right, even though this had led to three dead men. Even though nothing in this place would ever be the same again. In life there is no guilt that can escape the moment when it must be paid for. We pay for everything, always. Even within ourselves.

'Good morning...'

Glasses, hair sticking up, rain-sprayed trousers. He is carrying an old-fashioned student's briefcase, the kind you do not often see anymore. Cataldo had not heard him come in.

'I'm looking for Professor Lodi. Don Athos Lodi.'

He is a young priest, must be about twenty-five. Tall, slim, smiling. He is already very interested in the library – the warm colours of the shelves, the ivory of the books inviting one to pick them up, leaf through them. Is this what Don Lodi looked like at that age?

'I see. Who are you?'

'I'm sorry. My name is Ottavio Gatti, I'm from Como.'

'Looking for the Professor?'

'Yes.'

'Do you know him? Do you have an appointment?'

He shakes his head. 'No. But I've read a lot of his work...'

'Ah...'

'His essays. His research. That's why I'd like to meet him. Professor Nuzzi, from the Università Cattolica sent me.' He hesitates and then adds, 'I've written a thesis on Rebora and Tolstoy...'

'Do you speak Russian?'

'Yes, reasonably well...'

'Very interesting...'

'I've reworked it and I'd like to show it to him...'

'To have it published?'

'That's my dream... but it's not just that. I'd really like to know what he thinks of it.'

'Why?'

'Because the Professor is an exceptional scholar... he deals with things in an extremely sensitive way, and with great intellectual honesty. Yes. Honesty. That's what pervades his work. He must be like that in life as well.'

Cataldo looks at him without saying anything.

'Are you one of his assistants?' asks the young priest.

'In a way.'

He asks no more questions. He looks around.

'This is a nice place. I'd like to study here.'

So Cataldo puts his hand in his pocket. He offers the key, in his open palm.

'What's this?'

'You can wait for him here, if you want.'

He is surprised, taken aback. 'Thank you. So you think...'

'Yes, he'll be here,' he says, smiling. 'And I hope he likes your book.'

The young priest thanks Cataldo again as he leaves. Then he opens his case, pulls out a typescript and places it on the table. His heart is gripped by a mysterious trepidation, an indefinable excitement... something close to joy.